Thin's

Blues

Trini's Blues

And if you do not love yourself...

By B.A. Buie

Names: Buie, B. A., author.

Title: Trini's blues / B.A. Buie.

Description: Marietta, GA : Bianca Arrington, 2020.

Identifiers: LCCN 2020915475 (print) | ISBN 978-1-7355977-1-3 (paperback) | ISBN 978-1-7355977-2-0 (hardcover) | ISBN 978-1-7355977-0-6 (ebook) | ISBN 978-1-7355977-3-7 (audiobook)

Subjects: LCSH: Women--Fiction. | Women--Poetry. | Self-actualization (Psychology)--Fiction. | Self-actualization (Psychology)--Poetry. | Short stories. | Poetry. | BISAC: FICTION / Women. | FICTION / Short Stories (single author) | POETRY / Women Authors.

Classification: LCC PS3602.U34 T75 2020 (print) | LCC PS3602.U34 (ebook) | DDC 813/.6--dc23.

This is a retelling of events in the author's life. Some conversations and events have been recreated and/or supplemented. Some persons are composites based on the stories of more than one individual. The names and details of some individuals have been changed to respect their privacy.

For information about special discounts for bulk purchases please contact: email babuie.babuie.com or website www.babuie.com

Dedicated with love and admiration to my
beloved son and sacred daughter.
May you always find the courage to surrender to
your dreams and greatness.

Truth

In a twinkling of an eye
I was mesmerized by this guy
He snuck up on me like a spy
And now my womanhood is on Fiyaa

I like how he could keep his composure
Like a righteous soldier
When the battle first begun
He pulled his strength from the sun

Sista let yourself go
But I was too high to simply go with the
flow
My inner conscious was bleeding
Because I would not say no

As his dreads rustled in my ears
I released all fears
And this diamond turned to rock
As the rhythm he dropped blew up the spot

This brutha had me locked down
Pinned to his soft yet hard chest
As the Reds, yellows, and blues began to
spin
Our bodies got tangled in a mess

I confess, there is a crime being committed
Guilty as sin my mind, body, and soul were
involved in it.

My emotions grew wings and flew
With them went my conscious too
For certain this man knew
What his dance was bond to do

Mind you, the cypher was never completed
Both of us wore shackles that would
constantly come between us

That's why this mystery is dead, and his
absence is fucking with my head
I don't think you heard a word I said.
But I still got you wandering how what
began
Ended
So soon
So fast
So quickly
Was love

Love that cut till you could see the white meat while at the same time bandage seeping wombs you didn't even know existed. Making what was rotten, smell like mangoes.

"I believe that was Trini. ???",
"No seriously! That was him".

I know that tan hummer with tinted windows and chrome wheels anywhere. There it was creeping down memorial drive.

"Can't be",
"Maybe It's his brother"?

He supposed to be at work. Working the late shift. He took a job after the housing crash. Houses aren't selling and we can't keep renters, so my man is making sure we are all okay.

He's just a hard-working Trini boy. Nothing can come between him and his duty to his family. But let's follow him anyways. Just in case he ain't as hard-working as, I think.

And so, we did.

It was him and I am not myself. Not present in my body. Not available to anyone, not even my children. I am nothing, no one, I have nothing, no one.
Don't look at me!!
Don't see my pain. You don't deserve the joy of knowing that I failed.

I know you've been patiently waiting for a moment like this. To know that I am the most miserable of them all.

Don't look at me!

I should not have followed that truck. I should have stayed in the restaurant and finished my food.
Instead, I chose to know.
Knowing that ignorance is bliss.
Not knowing what bliss really is.
I chose to know.

So, we left hot plates of jerk chicken and oxtail in pursuit of fucking truth!
A truth that was irrelevant for so long. Truth made relevant by its witness.

She saw it too. She saw the truck and she knew he was not supposed to be in that place at that time.
She saw my face and she knew I knew too.

And so we MUST leave hot plates and pursue the truth.

I knew what lied in that parking lot. I knew who drove that truck and I knew what was going to happen.
I will not embarrass myself, but I will let the truth rise to the occasion that it's been waiting for.
But I will not embarrass myself.

I am his wife.

And she isn't.
She is skinny.
He doesn't like skinny girls.
She is sloppy.
He doesn't like sloppy girls.
She is light-skinned.
Wait, His baby mama is light-skinned.
But she wasn't his wife.
And this hoe obviously wasn't smart. What woman would lie and pretend she is related to a married man; she is obviously fucking.
Cousins? Cousins don't meet in the parking lot at 2am, wearing cologne. Cousins don't look concerned that his wife is approaching. I know cousins. I have cousins. We don't fuck!

There it was and there we were. All in this moment of truth. Picking sides and fighting for control. I had all the keys in my hand. The keys to the truck and to his freedom.

And his phone.

Why didn't I leave the truth there in the parking lot? I confirmed what I always knew, but it wasn't enough.
The taste of truth lingered on my tongue and I must have more, or it will continue to haunt me.
I just wouldn't be satisfied without knowing that I held the keys to his heart.

"he's so stupid"

Locked phone easily assessed by the first attempt. His name reversed.

"stupid"

I.N.I.R.T

"I'm in"

I wanted to see myself in his world. What do I look like? Am I kind and beautiful?
Am I the only one?
Well no, but am I the most important one?

I am his wife.

Truth is, in my world he is everything. He is beautiful. 6 feet with cocoa skin and floating locs. I imagined he had secrets inside of every coil and I wanted to know what exists in each.

Precious. Guarded.

What must be kept close to a crown so troubled and determined? Deep within rotating shafts that stretch pass every worry in search of something greater. Touching his constant, deep thought. Replaying every pain. Organizing and storing what is sacred.
I twist them with my healing hands. Seeing the beauty in each locs imperfection. Sensing their struggle for survival and helping them along the way. Continuing the rotation at the same time exploring his crown and feeling close to my king. Reading his stories told from strand to strand and hearing his soul cry. Taking care as he rests between my thighs.

He is beautiful.

Dark, mysterious eyes and grand cheekbones to the heavens. Pouty lips nested in the best goatee I've ever seen; outlining few words expressed with the deepest vibrato the human ear can hear.

Every smile so fresh and reassuring.
Every touch, strong and gentle.
Every hug safe.

So powerful, cause I knew it took a lot for joy to rise from his shallow graves marked by headstones etched with grief.

> **here lie a child's confidence and self-esteem**
> **here lies an absent father**
> **here lies an angry stepfather**
> **here lies a blind mother**
> **here lies a hungry and scared boy**

I don't mind kissing his feet and tasting salty skin, cause he shared that joy with me.
He brought me grapes and tea in the morning. He rubbed my back until infinity. He watched me as I slept and filled cups with warm coconut milk and sweet honey.
He is beautiful and he makes me feel royal. It's as if I sit upon a throne that lives in one of those locs. I am the fresh flowers on that headstone. Honoring his struggle. That expression of gratitude for the reward that be me.

Precious. Guarded.

But wait! Stop

Truth is

I wasn't in his locs. I am the fresh cut flowers left at the surface of shallow graves to wilt and die. In time becoming a part of the soil in which things are buried. A symbol of those left behind to suffer, while you slumber in peace and tranquility. The only music I hear is that of raindrops from the endless tears that poor from my brokenness

Truth is he didn't see me at all. I was not precious and guarded.
The only thing he guarded was in that phone where lies his precious conversations, pictures, and recordings. None of me. Just random freaks.

<u>Mu-Tha-Fucker!</u>

There is so much information in the truth. Too much information to process. I had to take a strategic approach to uncover it all. So, I began looking for what he covets in place of me.

The baby mama.

My intuition guided me as I navigated his world of scandals and lies. I could feel my bliss shrink with every touch of the screen. Every swipe is leading me further and further into unworthiness.

From
He doesn't see my beauty.
To
He doesn't see me at all.
To
I am not beautiful.
To
I am not worthy

Yet I continue tapping and reading. Discovering truth felt like playing your favorite record backward only to hear what you hate and what hates you.
Luther Vandross turns Anti-Christ
Bob Marley turns Politician
Lauren Hills' joy is not in Zion.
Erykah Badu is trying to convince me to eat pork.
John Coltrane's swift finger movements on the saxophone are throwing gang signs.
Aretha Franklin is being very disrespectful and yet I continue tapping and reading.

Learning that the truth is not what I believed.

She is naked and spread out like a beached West Indian whale. Suffering. Beaching itself as a last attempt to escape misery. Pretending that one big curve is enough.
One big curve that starts at her forehead and ends at her knee cap.
And her feet are so big. No toes. All puffy feet with the water retention of a dirty pond overcome with leeches, piss, and bacteria.
Stringy, flat hair.
Cut it! It's dead.

Paled skin. Bland. Absent. Empty. Hallowed pores. Not even the sun will touch that.
But he did.
Disgusting.
How did he ever?

I am everything.

My curves massage my body, like waves massaging the ocean floor. Finding the right time and place to swell, bend, and recede. Gracefully fortifying my sacred temple filled with hidden treasures.
Gold and knowledge. Creativity and Divinity.
My skin is as if the sunset created it and my hair full like the moon.
All pay homage to me as I pass. Wishing they could have what he has or be had by him.

She must have been working some of that West Indian voodoo. Mixing baths and sticking dolls. But nothing is in a picture. Everything is not enough, and I need to understand how. I need the story.

I must have the truth.

So, I continue to swipe and read, and in those lines, I found a place that he goes when he is not with me.
I found the 5-bedroom home with 3 1/2 bathrooms.
I found family pictures and celebrations with uncles, aunts, and grandparents.
I found truth

I found the legacy he built in my American name. Yes, my name, because he was mine and everything he had belonged to me.
The cars, the house, the name, his freedom belonged to me.

I am his wife.

It was me and my ancestors that sacrificed so that he could be free.
What about me? What about my freedom?
I stayed where I thought he wanted me to be. Close to his crown.
        Precious and guarded.
Safe.

But the truth is I'm not safe. I'm not Precious.
I'm guarded against the truth.
Kept within bliss, but outside of joy.

I am now pissed.

So, pissed that I began following the cookie crumbs to every woman he may have kissed, hugged, or inserted his little curry penis in.
Including any "distant relatives" or "cousins" who may have even considered it.
I'm dialing.
Introducing myself as his wife. Sharing with them some of my broken hearts' truth and how concerned I was for other women who may have been exposed to not only his lies but his H.I.V. It was my duty as a black woman to reach out and provide my Sista's with this important information.

To show them the courtesy per the sisterhood rooted in loyalty and respect.
Like a raging Umoja, on the first day of Kwanzaa, I am practicing unity. Helping my community. With dry tears and laughter in my glass of wine, I dialed those numbers and called in honor of my ancestors who seek to make what was wrong, right.

By any means necessary. I'm justified.

Yes, I'm burning each of these hoes as if they stood upon the kinara with tiny wicks coming out the top of their heads.
One by one I light them each and laugh as they cry out from the pain of fire and brimstone. Hot wax slides down from their heads carrying toxic thoughts, pass crusty lips, pass a dulled heart, pass a scared belly, down pass a dirty vagina, down pass loose legs onto paper memories set a fire by me.

Kujichagulia Bitches!

My ancestors chant as they dance in celebration around flames to the sound of the djembe in my head.

I served their lies, lies, and kept the truth for me.
It was mine too.
Mine to do with what I please.

They are not innocent victims in this matter.
Desperate but not innocent.
Nor are his family.

They all knew.
His father
His mother
His brothers
His sisters
His nieces and nephews
His baby mama.

They all played their part, while I carry the burden of their hopes and dreams. My heart is their community property. My womb the dumpsite for empty promises and ill intent. Yes, the path to my hell is paved with their good intentions. Brick by Brick they all worked to get what they know I am not willing to give. My soul. My very life they would have without concern of my children.

My legacy.

His children. They also knew and played. There will be no exception for the rot from which they spawn.

They can all be sent back on the banana boat that carried their rotten asses here. And he can go with them. They can float off into the sunset together. Let the sounds of steel pans carry them back to the sweet sound of gunfire and clashing machetes.

I called in sick to work just so I could stop them all.
I made a list of names, gender, and sizes.

I want them to be comfortable in their orange jumpsuits.
I paid the fees and filed the divorce papers.
I sat alone in the dark until I knew they all just wanted to be precious, guarded, and safe.

Until I knew the truth.

Truth is I would be alone again.

Genesis

I mourn through my tears
I cry through my poetry
I rise through my voice
I sing from my heart

My mama ran away when I was 5 years old. She was the only one who could see me and thought I was beautiful. I would be invisible until she came back home. No one would feel like singing as they brushed my hair and cook me grits. No one cared if my teeth were clean or my edges laid. No one would see pass the skin condition that prevented me from walking sometimes or the long scar left behind by a cyst, that peeped out just below my hairline.

No one.

No one would feel how weary I was in my silence.

Immature pain left to its own devices is imaginative and resilient.
while undisciplined emotions take many shapes.

Mine were many hollowed things.

The long-hollowed tunnel beneath the surface of a little black girls' soul.
The ceramic heart.
The echo filled attic and vacant basement.
A translucent smiling face.
A hot air balloon.
A tooth cavity.
The small void between two praying hands.
Plastic Easter Eggs and bells without jingle.
The shade of a lamp with no bulb.
Lego blocks and tissue boxes.
Giant ball-shaped hair barrettes held together by elastic bands.

Bands that refuse to let me wrap my ponytail one more time without giving into resistance. Taking instant flight. Slapping my knuckles and pinching the crouch between my thumb and index finger. Ushering deep pain to the surface. For a moment sending me back in time.
Reminding me of my mother before I could push the memories back down into their place.

A woman who filled hollowed churches with spirit.
Who congregated with melodic scripture. Then hummed it from the soles of her feet, up to her belly and out into cathedralic ceilings.

It was her voice that allowed bright rays to escape from outside, through painted glass and into the sanctuary where burgundy pews pointed at carpeted pathways decorated with white suites, white gloves, and collection plates.

Her voice gave sound to tears and shape to spirits.

Spirits that possessed people to dance and shout while liberated rays of light explored the pulpit before exposing a giant white, blue-eyed Jesus.
I there wondering why he was there, and what is he doing? He is obviously not studying us. But us studying him, waiting for something.
Why not put mama up there?

It's was her voice that translated ancient words printed on thin sheets with golden trim and stains of oil so we all could receive their lessons.

I can't tell you what Matthew or John said, but mama said...
"If anybody asked"
"where I'm going"
"If anybody wants to know"
"where I'm going"
"I'm going up a yonder to be with my Lord"

4 years later they claimed her bones were found deep in the woods. They say she was like me.

Alone.

All that time, she was less than a mile away, resting against the backside of a tree. Resting until the cold slowed her breathing to a complete stop. Daydreaming about another world they said only existed in her mind. A world without daughters or husbands, sisters or brothers, mothers, or fathers.

Hollowed.

Where they spoke in silence with bright watery eyes and overexuberant forced smiles.
They said her world was dark and motionless. Overcrowded with thoughts, preventing movement. Void of reality.
One where she didn't need warm clothes, food, or money. They said she laid a black plastic bag with all she had down in my grandfather's backyard before laying her burdens down against that tree. How does one get out of their mind when your mind is in you?

That's when I knew I was invisible for real. Cuz If she knew I was here, if she could see me, she would have been back. She would not let me exist without song and afro puffs. Grits and chicken. Fluoride. She would want to know that I laid my face to the prayer rug and talked to God before bed. She would want to know that my skin is clean and rubbed with medicine. That cocoa butter had been massaged into my scar and Crisco behind my knees. She must can't see me. I've been too quiet. Too invisible.

Sitting under the tent. My legs were swinging from the chair as all the grown-ups said goodbye to my mother who was supposedly in a gold-plated jar. I look down. All I see are my knees and grass until a black patent leather shoe with a white ruffled sock folded over the top of it swings up into sight. Quickly disappearing just before the other appears. I'm entranced by their coordination and motion.

They swing.
Right knee, grass, black patent leather shoe with white ruffled sock folded over top of it.
Left knee, grass, black patent leather shoe with white ruffled sock folded over top of it.

I rather watch them versus grown-up tears and forced smiles. "It's a celebration of life" they say. But not my Grandma Isabell. She says, "it's a beginning, not an end". And her warrior's eyes stand guard over my sister and me. Ready to take down the tribe of Buie for the sake of her son and granddaughters. And so stand

Grandma Isabell's children... (My daddy) Johnny-Mack, Mae, Becca, Miss Ann, Poot, Ray Jr, Fran, Robert, Lianne, Pearl, Ester, Angel, Alicia, Kat, Nelle. Them and their husbands. Them and their wives.

And so stands Grandpa Ludie and his children. Bernice, Darwin, Debra, Caroline. Them and their husbands. Them and their wives. Outnumbered but still ready to defend mama's honor.

All honoring the moment with sanctity and respect. Preparing for whatever may come after this day was over and the war could resume.
Who gets the children?
The house?
The furniture in the house?
The shrunk?
The prayer rug in the shrunk?
The car?
The clothes?
Whose fault is it?
Who broke her heart?
Who broke her spirit?
Who turned their back?
Who closed their eyes?
Who left her alone?
Who? Who? Who?

Hollowed.

I knew the truth. She's not in there. There? In a jar? Nor was she in the woods? Neither are up yonder, and that's where she always said she

was going.   So, I knew she wasn't in that jar. The choir knew the truth too as they sang. "Hallelujah, Hallelujah. We're going to see the king".
They said "We". All of Us. Me. Mama. All of Us.

Just now I knew she would show up with new hairdo and fresh clothes.   I imagined all the kids at school being jealous as the girl they pitied was checked out early by Whitney Houston. *Turns out she was hiding under an alias all that time. And I the mystery child from the tabloids. She pulls up in a stretch limousine. Steps out and a red carpet unravels from the limo door all the way up to the school entryway. Lights flashing. The principle greets her with a smile and handshake.*

"Welcome back Mrs. Buie, I mean Mrs. Houston"

wink wink

"Right this way"

She finds me sitting alone in a noisy classroom. Quietly working.
An Angel.
She recognizes me and immediately starts running to me with her arms out.

"Mama!! I knew you would be back"

I fall into her arms.

"Grab your stuff. You're done here."

Fans line the sidewalk as I skip with my hand in hers. Waving goodbye forever.
Her eyes sparkled like diamonds. The whitest teeth I have ever seen.
And she smells so clean and fresh. Brand new.

"Mama, what about my sister?"
"She's staying with your dad"

Blinding camera flashes and deafening clicks.
I'm happy

Legs swinging.
Right knee, grass, black patent leather shoe with white ruffled sock folded over top of it.
Left knee, grass, black patent leather shoe with white ruffled sock folded over top of it.

Let's eat!

I pop down from the chair and into the crowd. Quietly listening as many speculated many things about her disappearance. Trying to ignore the itch from the grass.

Time passed and people moved on. Daddy was married and divorced. I entertained myself in a mansion as he and my sister forgot about me. Leaving no one to tell me how diseased, ugly or stupid I was. I could sing as loud as I wanted too and dance from room to room without interruption. Video games and movies all day. Instant cheese grits with bacon pieces and pizza. popcorn ceiling gazing carpet angels. Bike rides from the kitchen to the dining room, down the

hallway, around to the living room, through the den, and back to the kitchen. Pillow rides down the stairs. Kissing barbie and ken dolls. Frying bologna in the easy bake oven. Taking a ride on the garage door as it climbs up from the ground. Discovering Daddies guns and porno movies on VHS.
Bubble baths in the jacuzzi. Musicals starring cabbage patch kids. More pizza.

Faded memories were eventually replaced with bigger and bigger fantasies. Some too big to take with me to Grandma Isabell's house. A few weeks with Grandma forced me out of my crab shell and into a world where I did not belong. Where I felt crammed and ridiculous. Suffocated by all their shame and pity. The constant greeting of shaking heads and hugs dimmed my light. I could only shine in my world in ways they would not understand. A voice that no one hears. A dance that no one here sees. A place where I was mesmerizing to the unsuspecting audience that sees me and is amazed by my rhythm and notes. The more they watch, the higher I jump, the louder I sing. All too big for Grandma's house.

Cheese eggs, sausage, biscuits, and molasses. Watermelon and tomatoes off the vine. Soup with neckbones. Field peas and cornbread. Chocolate cake.

She could never convince me to go outside and play with the other kids. I don't like the outside. it's hot out there and heat makes my skin itch.

And so do flies. So, I sat in the rocking chair and listened. Listened to everything. The phone calls. The conversations with neighbors. The pots clinging. The hogs snorting. The kids yelling. The trucks honking as they flew by. The toilets flushing. The screen door slamming shut. The hurt cry. The rocking chair squeaking. The switch hissing. The hurt cry again. The windchime ringing. Eventually, Grandma would come, and we would watch the news and soap operas. Between that and daddy's porno's I knew all about life and how the real world was.

One day Grandma Isabell came in and sat down with a big brown envelope. Inside a letter from my mother and newspaper clippings. The letter was a handwritten farewell that I never knew existed.

I love you. Goodbye. Please give these gifts to my girls.

"Your granddaddy prolly took the gifts", Grandma Isabell rambled.
Grandma Isabell always had words.
"took everything she had. Didn't leave y'all nothin!"

The article told a story of remains found.
Missing Beauty Queen, Songstress, Salon owner, and Ex-wife of entrepreneur.
Identity confirmed by dental records.
No evidence of foul play.

I know these things from the TV.   These things are real.

I go back to the letter.
I read it again and again, trying to find hidden meaning in a few words.
Maybe everything is the opposite?

No, No, No!!   Because if Goodbye is hello then love is hate and my mother does not hate me.

Does she?
Did she run away from me?

I rock and think.

She is discovered in a hospital. Amnesia.
She doesn't know who she is. She sees me and her memory returns. Instantly!
I brush her hair.
I wash her feet.
I feed her soup.
I sing her songs.
And she is back, and I am no longer invisible.   We are no longer alone.

Back home, alone I lay in bed, thinking.   The house is dark and silent.   The air is still. Coldness.
It would not let me sleep.   No matter how I told my story, I could not get it to fit with this new information.

Goodbye
Dental records confirmed identity.

No evidence of foul play.

I tossed and turned. I'm hot. I'm cold. It just doesn't make any sense.
Yonder not in the woods. Yonder not in the jar. Where the hell is Yonder?

Goodbye
Dental records confirmed identity.
No evidence of foul play.

Heavy was the information on my head. I couldn't hold it in.
Clenching my teeth and squeezing my eyes closed.
My back ached. My stomach cramped.
Pulling my own hair, Tossing, turning, fighting.
Pushing it down, down deep into those hollow spaces.
Chest burning.
I was going to explode. It had to be released.
But I didn't want to let it go.

She has a twin, same teeth.
Teeth replaced during accident.
Conspiracy.
Grandpa Buie hiding her for money.
She's in his house.

Then I saw her. As if the buried memory from the past was now, at that moment with me. And I saw her. Right there.
The last smile, that said,
"I love you", "Goodbye"

She reached out to hand me something, but I couldn't reach back far enough.
Before I knew it, she was walking away.

Gone.

Faded into nowhere.
In an instant, I knew the truth.
"MAMA!!" Started echoing in those hallowed walls. Eventually exploding like a raging volcano from my mouth.
It hurt like hell. Shaking my entire self uncontrollably.
I vomit with my tears. Releasing it all. Toxic waste poured out from my body. It hurts. Paralyzing pain.
I'm dying too. I'm dying too. I'm cold. I'm deep in those woods. I'm on the backside of that tree. I'm laying it all down.

Gone.

I awake to the whitest sunlight I've ever seen. Virgin rays floated above my head. I reach up to grab dancing particles and watch my fingers move in euphoria.

Love only leads to pain. Pain is numbing. Ignorance is bliss.

The beginning

Closed

It was time I abandoned the house and begin my search to find whatever she may have been looking for.
A voice.
A purpose.
A way of being what I'm supposed to be.
Whatever that is.

I fueled my search with poetry, song, dance, art, and fashion.

Sometimes I found it with my Mom's youngest sister, Donna, where there where afros, Toni Morrison, braids, djembes, frankincense, Ntozake Shange, mud-cloth, locs, love and light. Other times I found it while sitting on a barstool in the back of my Dad's club watching the Temptations, Latimore or Bobby Blue Bland perform.

At times drag racing in my charcoal grey Nissan 280ZX turbo with leather interior, tinted windows, and T-Tops.

Other times I found it in freaknik traffic or at Magic City where my sister and her friends worked. Sometimes it was in daddy's girlfriend's spaghetti.

One day I found it in a documentary about Angela Davis who said, "we have to talk about liberating minds as well as liberating society." Another day it was Scarlet who taught me that all emotions and things will eventually be Gone with the Wind, so manage your expectations accordingly.

I was Dorothy in The Wiz and Carmen's Dorothy at the same time. Tempting hearts and leaving behind disappointments as I eased on down the yellow brick road in search of a wizard to take me home.

Sometimes in my voice on stage singing Soweto! Soweto! Soweto!
Sometimes as I stand on a rooftop screaming "fuck the police"!!!
Sometimes sitting quietly with my reflection.

One place I never found it was in high school. Sprayberry High, where shallow minds grow into shallower minds. Where young privileged white kids are coached to pass state exams. Where being black is hated but cool.
Where the football team never wins, and cheerleaders lack spirit and rhythm. Where lunch tables are segregated by race, color, cuteness, and class. Where curvy virgins like me where labeled hoes and outcasted while the real hoes were popular.

Where I knew I was not supposed to be.

At the time I thought I was supposed to be on the southeast side of Atlanta. In Decatur. Riding with my T-tops off and music blasting. That's where I found my first prom date. He was smooth and gentle. He looked at me as if I were the prettiest thing he had ever seen. In the purest way possible. He bared his soul to me. No catcalls, or whistles. No "Hey SHAWTY!" No groping! Always a gentleman. Always a friend. He listened to my poetry and loved to hear me sing.
What do you think of this?
How do you feel about that?

He laughed at my silly jokes and saw the innocence beneath my seductive shell. He never took advantage. He held it high.

I always thought he was too good for me. I'm not worthy. Can't you see I'm closed?

School wasn't his thing either.

He (we) loved doing our own thing and cars. We rode around in a cherry red convertible impala with white interior, whitewall wheels, and classic rims listening to Goodie Mob. He restored that car after buying it from the junkyard. It took every dime he made under the shade tree and weeks of sweat equity, but he did it. And we spent hours in that car. Just driving around saying hey to his Maw Maw and Uncles. Hanging out at the park where our feet never touched the ground. We would stop at this shady Chinese restaurant in the parking lot of the flea market to eat fried rice and chicken wings. Then we'd gaze out over the city from stone mountains top, talking about our dreams while he drank from the brown paper bag his uncle slipped him. He told me no matter what he would be there.

And he was.

Whenever I called, he came. Whether to bleed my clutch or pull me out of my head and back into the real world. He was there. He was there when I was getting jumped at the skating rink. To listen to my pain. He was always there. And when it was time for prom, and no one asked me, there he was. Looking like a chocolate pimp in his ivory tux, twisted hair, and gator boots.   He looked so good. I loved his smile. That big and genuine heart shined through his whole self. Especially his eyes. Like paradise, they left me without worry and in complete solace. Beautiful twinkling black prisms like many suns and many moons, dancing behind waterfalls. My red gown. His red bowtie. That impala. We were fresh. We could only bear the prom for 10 minutes or so, before escaping back to The Dec where we watched a movie at the drive-in.

We kissed.

He took me home.

He told me he loved me.

I was closed.

He didn't care, when I called, he still came.

To replace my fender before my dad found out that I was drag racing again or to the theatre to see me perform.

He was there and I was never alone.

Never feeling like a burden or pitied.

He was honored. I was searching.

Closed.

The streets were always jealous. Jealous of his swag and beauty. Jealous of his vision. Jealous of his potential.   Jealous that he had a mother and father who loved him.

But not even the will of a two-parent home could overcome the lure of Atlanta's eastside gangs. Eventually, he would become affiliated. The closer he got to the gang the further away he pushed me.

Still, when I called, he came.
Even when my boyfriend beat my ass.
He showed up to my black eye, busted lip, and bruised ribs.
He packed my bag and took me to his Maw Maw.
They nurtured my wounds, introduced me to an iron skillet then sent me back to the northside where good girls like me belonged.

The ride home was quiet. He had a lot on his mind and so did I.
He tucked me in and slept on the couch until the shade tree called.

Sometimes I found it in selfish moments like these when all I could see was me.
When my pain was so close to the surface that I could really feel it.
And it was so loud. Obnoxious.
I could do nothing but manage it until it was back under control.
Unable to distract me from my search.

Other times it was in selfish acts of humility.
Like the day I called to check on him and say thank you only with the intent of luring him back into our friendship after ignoring him.

He was still open.

We reminisced and laughed. Just like old times.
He told me about a baby on the way.
I asked if he was in love.

Gag. Exhale. Click.

One moment we were two friends talking, the next he was gagging, exhaling. Click.

Me assuming it was foolish boys roughhousing, I called back. The voicemail answered. I yelled at the recording in hopes that the entire house could hear me. "Y'alls need to grow up! And turn that music down!"

The next day I called. His mother answered. "Honey he's not here, dead. He's gone. He's not coming back".

Sometimes I found it where time froze and the world paused, giving me a moment to sort things out.

Everything has its place. The doors were closed, and there was no room. I decided to remove the loneliness and silence from storage, making room for this new sorrow and new grief. But where to put the guilt and shame? Where to put the selfishness and regrets? Where to put my friend? Somewhere that it won't get gone in the wind.

Apart of me grateful I was closed. How would I manage the infiltration of more pain into my being?
Another part of me wondering how our lives would have been had we...Had I not been closed. So much to sort out.

The detective said what I heard was not roughhousing, but him struggling from his throat being slit during a robbery. The exhale, his last. The click, the phone cord cut.

His mother found him at the end of that long telephone cord that wound from the kitchen, down the hallway, and into his bedroom. The only thing missing was a big-screen TV.

Closed

Fear

It wasn't long before I found myself back to enjoy a good physical fight.
I believed I needed to be dragged back into this world or else I might disappear like my mother.
Find myself drifting into nowhere.
So, I hold on, even when he's beating my ass or gifting me with an STD from a trashy white girl.

He. We weren't always like this.
I saw something he couldn't see in himself. Something bigger than his six-foot-two Shaka Zulu frame. Deeper than his sienna toned skin and wavy hair. Sexier than his New York accent, leather jacket, baggy jeans, Newport's, and timberland boots. Heavier than the cross around his neck. I saw. I had comfort, a friend, a partner. Someone to dance with. To play with. Someone to sleep with and run with. Someone to write with. We wrote poetry together. Taking turns, finishing each other's phrases. Reading them out loud and celebrating hysterically the moment when profound sense, rhyme, and genius met. He had mastered the English language. His wisdom, my creativity made beautiful notes. In our own little world, we made magic.

Every kiss was like the first time. Watching me, watching him. Pulling me in until our lips met. Introducing tender bites and tongue. Every combination, unique. He unlocked something in me that I did not know existed.

In my presence, his lap was never empty. His chest, never cold. We had to touch. We had to acknowledge the connection. We had to dance. We had to hike deep into the woods and high into the hills. We had to make love ova and ova again.

There is a constant series of silent implosions happening in my soul. The best distraction from everything and I don't want to do anything else.

It was I who looked for him in the crowd at the skating rink.

Eye contact.
He's mine.

Just after numbers are exchanged, I feel a hard blow to the back of my head.

Sprayberry hoes.

I held onto his number, while at the same time preparing to defend myself.

I held onto his number as I slipped and fell to the ground.

I held onto his number as I kicked and spun in circles on my back.

I held onto his number as handcuffs asphyxiated my wrist.

I held onto his number as I was dragged out of the skating rink.

I held onto his number as I acknowledged being banned, agreeing never to return.

I held onto his number as my "affiliated friends" from Decatur finished the fight as I cheered from across the street.

I held onto his number as the car sped off to meet up with my friends at the International house of Pancakes.

I held onto his number until I had a moment to etch it into my memory for safekeeping.

He's mine.

Wasn't long before he was experimenting with my body, living in my father's home, and driving my car. He totaled my charcoal grey 280ZX turbocharged Nissan with T-tops. I got a hot red Jeep Wrangler with 10-inch speakers encased in plexiglass. He eventually wrecked my red Jeep Wrangler too.

But I, We didn't want to do anything else

It also wasn't long before I realized how irresponsible and unmotivated, he was.

I still didn't want to do anything else.

Hours pon hours of cypher laced with purple haze in green pastures. Browns and yellows colliding as we make love to Afro-soul house mixes and Maxwell.

I, we didn't want to do anything else.

We moved into our own place. He cooked. I paid bills. We argued. He hit me in my face. A golf ball grew on my temple. A crack in my ribs. The police carried him away. I destroyed his only things. His stereo and sofa.

I, We still didn't want to do anything else.

Some girl called for him while Nas played on the boombox. I heard everything. I complained. He body-slammed me into the carpet angels we made where his sofa use to be. The police carried him away again.

I still didn't want to do anything else.

He returned to the safest space he knew. Not with the father he just met, or the body where his mother used to be before giving her whole self to the streets. Back with his grandmother and grandfather in New York.

It was death that put me on the bus to see him. The absence of friend and lover was a lonely I could not bear. I needed a distraction. I needed to feel good. I needed to know that I was not alone. I needed what we once had.

So, Lauren Hill, Mary J. Blige, Jodeci, yes we all got on the bus with my poetry book in hand.

Twenty-one Hours provided plenty of time to reminisce about his surprise birthday party at my father's club. Stage lit and mike in hand freestyling like he on the corner with Mob Deep. Stage diving like a white celebrity.

Twenty-one hours provided plenty of time to daydream about meeting his grandparents in person for another birthday surprise. I imagined meeting them would be like a coming home. His grandmother was always so loving and welcoming over the phone. Their relationship was something I admired. The affinity he had for them both was always evident. He always bragged about her cooking and how much fun he had fishing with his grandfather. I could hear his grandmother smiling as we talked and planned my trip.

She didn't want us to do anything else either.

Not long after my arrival grandma was picking me up from the bus stop. Me in my distressed blue jean overalls and a tank top, with a sweatshirt tied around my waist and braids piled up on the top of my head. She in her animal print valor jogging suite, salt n pepper fade, shades, and gold rings on every finger.

Big hug.

All four windows in the Cadillac were down. I knew that Temptations song and so did she, and she wanted everyone in upstate New York to know that we were listening to that Temptation's song right now. Some of them knew it too! That's why they turned and commenced to singing and dancing as we came flying down the street.

Music blasting and cigarette ashes flying. Cutting corners and jumping curbs. So fast that I couldn't blink without missing a block.
All I could do was hold on and listen as she cussed out everybody.

The man in the blue Honda. "Get out the way Mutha-Fucka"

The teenage girl in the crosswalk. "Shit, Yo ass must ain't got no-mutha-fuckin were to be"

The church lady shaking her head while we waited for the light to turn green. "What the hell is wrong with you"

The street. "Fuckin Potholes"

God. "Asshole"

We arrived and it was not what I pictured. This was not like The Spike Lee Movies. Yes, there are brownstones with stoops and sidewalks, but no one is on them. No little girls playing hopscotch in the street. No double-dutch. No basketball. Just brownstones with sheets for curtains. Some with boarded-up windows. And trash. Streetlights accompanied by police cameras

"You big pussy!"
The old man getting out of the car parked in front of her house with a handicap plate.

"shhhiiiittttt"

And stairs. Lots of stairs. Up to the front door. Up to the kitchen. Up to the bedroom where I waited quietly and made note of the darkness inside. The stuff. The photo albums and mason jars, the tools and appliances, the baby dolls and newspapers, the ashtrays and water bed, the clothing and plastic containers, the radio, another radio, another radio and record player, the vinyl and cassettes, the portraits and candy dish, the stack of cards, another ashtray, The stack of bibles and T.V, The pliers and foil, Towels and Christmas décor, Lysol and clocks. Lots of clocks. The expired calendar and stuffed animals, tissue box and candles, cans of Campbell's chicken noodle soup, cigar boxes, and empty bottles. Stacked, placed, resting, landed, left everywhere.

I hear his voice and I'm scared. Maybe he doesn't want me here? Maybe I've been the distraction? Maybe he would be making beats and writing rhymes? Maybe he would be signed if not for me? Maybe he wants to do something else? Maybe he already did it? Maybe I should not have come?

Moments later I am in his arms and he is apologizing, and he is still mine.

We laid naked and sweaty in his waterbed, watching the stars as he inhaled a Newport and blew smoke out the window. He talked and I listened for hours. Sharing the unimaginable. Confessing that the sins of his grandparents far outweighed the sins of his parents. The house I lay naked in was actually a house of horrors. The place where his innocence was stolen and his anger was born. A torture chamber buried deep in his story that I was hearing for the first time.

At the time, I was unaware that the pandora's box had indeed been opened. There was serial like emotions, cynical pain, and ragging madness seeping from behind a beautiful mask that he could no longer wear. Yes, there were confessions of love and apologies and more poetry,

but maybe I want to do something else now?

Maybe he sensed it?

Nevertheless, I convinced him to quit his job and return home to me. He needed to be saved and I could do it. If my mother and I could lay our burdens down, so could he. And together we could continue to search. But he couldn't do anything else, and he didn't want me to do anything else either? He couldn't find work with his record; he couldn't take care of himself. He couldn't leave his abuse and neglect in New York.

One day while I was at work, he got frustrated sitting and trying to process everything, so he started carrying armfuls of my stuff to the river behind our apartment. That was something he could do. He could make me feel what I already felt.

Alone.

It started with clothes, hair products, and toiletries. It then escalated to jewelry. From there pots, pans, and food. Then furniture, my TV, paintings, and wallpaper made from bamboo. All carried down to the riverside and eventually into the river. I came home to an empty apartment. He and everything I owned was gone. I couldn't imagine where he could possibly put everything. I searched the entire complex.

Nothing.

I sat with my legs crossed looking out the patio window. Watching the night as if it could help me. I lay back, close my eyes, and begin to wave my legs back and forth across the carpet. Imagining I was back at my father's house making carpet angels. For a moment opening my eyes to gaze at the ceiling. Then closing them again. Opening them once more, but this time looking back out the window, where he stood. Head against the glass, smiling for a moment. Then glaring as if his eyes where his hands and they were wrapped around my throat, slowly choking me to death. I froze. I couldn't move. I couldn't scream. Is this what mama found on the cold back side of that tree? How fitting it would be for me to find the same thing.

Trapped in my apartment, I couldn't do anything but sit there until after he slowly walked away.

I want to do anything else but this.

I don't want to die. I don't want to see him die in jail. I don't want to be here anymore.

After a few days of seeing him everywhere. Him, sitting in the distance as I arrived home from work. His love notes left underneath the windshield wiper of my car. Him, taping on my bedroom window at 3am. Him, paging me ova and ova again from different numbers.

I left and went to work at my father's bar. In the northern, discreet country town of Hapeville where I found something else to do.

There was a bush in Hapeville. In that bush, there was refuge and terror unlike I ever known.

But I had to do something else.

I wanted to be safe, so I ran into the bush.

Fearless

All is sacred here.
Here in this place where seeds are planted,
and roots are prepared.
Introduce consciousness to flesh and breath
spirit into being.
Send fire and earth as a shield. Water and
electricity as a catalyst.
Take care oh sacred womb and let your
work go undisturbed.
Let not this world penetrate your sweet
haven.

All is kind here.
Here in this place where love is born, and
worries are non-existent
Give wisdom to creativity and let
understanding be infinite.
Bring all your powers to manifest peace out
of pain and joy out of fear.
Take care oh kind womb and let your work
go undisturbed.
Let not this world penetrate your sweet
haven.

All is blessed here
Here in this place where God just is, and
forgiveness is not necessary.
Allow your beloved creation to become an
altar.
Raise it up in purifying light and love.

Take care oh blessed womb and let your
work go undisturbed.
Let not this world penetrate your sweet
haven.

Let the transition and life honor you, oh
sacred womb. Glory.

I believe we choose the experience we want before entering the womb.
He chose vengeance.
Retribution for a prior life's wrongdoing.
And he came with fist, sword, and a thirst for validation.

With the right recipe, a mother's womb can heal and redirect any amount of pain.
Nine months of love, nourishment, gratitude, peace, and service to an internal alter could manifest amnesty.

Grace.

All she had was brokenness.

He chose well.
He knew that womb would not get in the way of his agenda. He had battlefield will and cunning strategy.

Genius.

The fight started at conception; it would not end. Every ounce of him aligned to one agenda, making him the most powerful man I ever knew. Even his skin fought the sun. Wining it lay torched and purged of any flaws. An impenetrable blanket rested pon an unbreakable West Indian frame. Ancient wisdom and unnerving temperament crowned in big, untamed locs.
Keen awareness and foresight nested in mesmerizing eyes.

The most sophisticated weaponization of God's child.
Long in stature and life.

He would live forever. He would fight forever.

Vindicated by the purpose established long before getting into that womb.

He never hesitated, he just knew what to do and did it.
Blood was a part of the battle and with that came familiarity. He remembered it from the womb. It belonged here. He was not alarmed by its presence. It spilled and he was reassured that he was doing exactly what he came here to do.

Many were attracted to his power. He was like the Angel Gabriel, vengefully beautiful.
He glowed. He preached. They listened.

Adored and feared, he was.

He had a hypnotizing aura. It was like standing in the darkest room with tiny specs of light exploding and dancing around. Like fireworks, captivated you stay, watching these cherubs fly and move about the space. Not knowing that sunlight would eventually fill that dark space, unveiling reality. Not cherubs, but sparks from bullets exiting guns and piercing bodies. You rub your eyes in disbelief of the Carnage now filling the space where you stand. And there he stands unbothered and justified.

I sought, I found protection. His love surrounded me in a fortress where nothing and no one could touch me.

Nothing else mattered.

Mercy.

Our first moments could not have been any more perfect. He spoke to me in an enchanting rhythm. In an angelic tone, he quoted the bible, taught me about Rasta-man ways and beliefs. He taught me to eat for my livity, not for satisfaction. He cooked vegan meals while we listened to Capelton, Jacob Miller, Israel Vibrations, and Bob Marley. He smoked pounds of herb while carving jewelry, pendants, and walking canes from wood. He looked at me with admiration and beauty. He let me dance. And when I pointed my toes and hands to the heavens, he let me see his smile, which was rare. He only let a few near me. They loved us and we loved them. No one would go hungry, and no one would be hurt as long as I was around.

For a moment he let me distract him from his purpose. For a moment he entered my sacred space and he put swords down. For a moment he did not fight. He loved.

For a time, he considered another possibility. What if life was not vengeful or bleeding? What if I could live without fighting?

I climbed into a bush filled with thorns and was safe as long as I stayed in my place.

The moment I moved; I was cut. Getting out would leave me with rupturing, deep wounds, but what mother wouldn't risk it all to save their child.

Glory

Something changed in me when life entered my womb. I found a whole new purpose.
I believed he would too, but he just refused to let go of his vengeance.
Instead, it escalated and he felt further justified.

"My youth need......"

no one was safe. No one.
Not friends, family, neighbors, corner store grocery workers.
Not mothers or fathers.
Not children or pregnant women.
No one was safe.

Not even me.

At first, I thought I could save him. If only I stepped into his world for a moment, maybe I could pull him out to safety.

So, I dodged cherubs and bullets.
I dispersed pieces of the gun across a 5-mile radius.
I dropped the bag and picked up the cash.
I paid the attorney fees.
I testified.
I kept my mouth shut.

My attempts to argue with destiny failed and as my belly grew, so did my concern for what was inside.

I was out of time. This bush is not my shield. It's my torture chamber.

Realizing my love in any form wasn't enough, I left just as our man child entered this world.

His rage used my body to create holes in walls.

His rage tied me up.

His rage bloody my face.

His rage invaded my sacred womb.

His rage awoke a rage in me. Rage like I've never known. Fearless rage. Mothering rage.

A rage that lifted him off his feet and threw him across the room.

I called my ancestors and they came.

Together, we whooped his ass.

Blind rage ignored the returning blows and continued to fight.

I would not lose.

I did not hesitate.

I just knew what needed to be done and did it.

Victory.

For the first time, I saw fear in his eyes. He had met his match.

I was stronger than him.

I saw the monster and was unafraid. I was now justified too.

And unbothered.

Unbothered by the beast before me, and the damage those thorns in that bush would do.
My flesh had been dragged; my womb, violated.
So, what if these thorns and briar tear and rip at me as I climb out.

What is blood to me? What is pain to me?

Bodies rained around as he dropped bombs on an already burning bush.
I emerged a warrior only to find my belly full again.

One on my hip and one inside of me, we walked towards a warming sun.

His Destiney was not ours.

They chose me and I chose them.

Mercy.

Love

Sometimes you just have to know that everything will be alright.

I pick up my bag and place it on back.
I pick up my daughter and secure her to my chest with strong material.
I pick up my sons' hand and secure it in my palm.
Precious and Guarded we march towards our own destiny.

My son made one look back then faced forward, while my daughter's gaze lingered over my shoulder.
Holding on to his unbothered fatherless shell long after it had faded into the distance.
But I,
Me,
My Body,
My Soul does not linger or look back. Not for a moment.

Barefoot and battered I marched onward with my precious cargo, gracefully stepping over bodies as if they were misplaced stones on my path.
quietly placing each step in its proper place.
Right, where it belonged.
Letting dangers find their way around me as I proceed without hesitation.
The battlefield still warm beneath my feet as something bigger and even more powerful than me deploys my warrior instincts to protect and guide us.
Each transition smooth and fluent.
It's Alvin Ailey meets my avatar, Neytiri.
I feel no fear, no pain.

And my prayers are seemingly instantly granted.

So do not disturb my peace.
I will shoot first and ask questions later.
The freedom chant within me can easily be turned into a warrior's chant to break you.

Do not disturb my peace and let me march on for your life's sake.

I hear nothing but what I need to hear.
I see nothing but what I need to see
I know nothing but what I need to know.

But for a moment I wonder, is this the place where mama went?
Is this what she was looking for?
This place where she forgot about me and my sister?
Where her love was pure yet unaccountable.

I did not want to be here.

The surviving heat of war warms my back and propels me forward, while my desire to save my children from violence, food deserts, redlined slums, and poverty pulls from the other side.

I, we march on.

I had changed and been granted grace by many sacrifices.
Some apparent. Others I did not even know of.
Some by those who had come and gone long before I got into Mama's womb.
Some unknowingly working today to prepare a place for us tomorrow.

I, we were covered in its blood as I found my way out of my head.
I just knew what to do and did it.

Maintaining a laser focus as the world around me crumbles into nothing and his battle continues in the far. Far. Far. Far distance.

Hope appears in the form of fire, burning in the sky and inside of me.

I'm tired.
Not weary, just tired.
But the sun feels so good and I just want to be closer to it.
So, I drop the bag.
I pick up my son and secure him to my back with strong material.
And continued to march until the land ends and the ocean begins.
We then took flight, landing on the Holy Cross.
In the twin city of Christiansted, Saint Croix, the Virgin Islands where we find rest for our tired souls. Safety in his own homeland. The place where his feet first felt dirt. The first place that love failed to make him chose something else. The one place he could never go.

Deep inhale through nose.

   Thank you, creator, for the mercy, grace, and love you have shown my children and me.

Deep exhale through mouth.
   We will honor you.

I spent my days working and my nights cooking, ironing pleats into their uniform, and packing lunches.
Bathing in the beach.
Laundry and grocery shopping on Saturday.
Church on Sunday.
Reading,
Reading,
Studying,
Studying,
Meditating,
Meditating,
Focused.

I'm sitting cross-legged watching lizards play in the rafters. Listening to reggaeton from the China man next door.
Smelling curry and hearing wildlife rejoice in the warmth of morning. Horses trotting and breadfruit pouncing against the steel roof. Like thunder, it rolls down crashing to the ground asking to be dinner.
Feeling the salty ocean breeze find my wounds and massage the heat from my neck.
The children run barefoot between the trees, picking up plumbs and eating as they laugh.
Throwing the seeds down wherever they finish.

Little Cruzan voices chant at the forefront of nature's constant song.
It's as if their words dance
"ma-me!"
"watch here ma-me"

They both hold tight to a thick rope tied around the thick arm of a mango tree. My daughter rests her feet on a big knot close to the end.
While my son runs and kicks his feet up to join hers just before the rope gets too far away from the ground.

There smiles and laughter are charged by the ropes swinging motion. Fearless they hold on as they fight against gravity. For a moment winning as they swing up, up towards the ocean above. In the following moment losing as they are dragged back down towards the earth. Only to win again just before running smack into it. Then lose again and win again until they are all exhausted.

Fearless

"I see y'all"

One by one I take each loc in my hand, slowly tracing my fingers up along its uneven surface until I feel virgin hair.
Hair that had yet to be caught up in the past. Like my children, touched, but not caught up and willing to start a new chapter. To write a new story.
With a slice of the scissors, I let it fall into my lap.
Loc by loc I release the pain I've been carrying. One by one I remove dead weight and feel my head become lighter and less burdened.
Moment by moment I ask for forgiveness and redemption in a sharp whisper.

Breath by breath I say thank you.

Some people save their locs. I burned mine with white sage and threw the ashes in the trash where they belonged.
Once the purifying fire took trapped tragedies and reveled the many lessons, there was no need to hold onto them.
I repeatedly open my arms wide and move them to hug the bellows of smoke as they rose from the flames, waving the lessons towards my eyes, nose, and mouth with my hands.

Inhaling and taking them all in.

Feeling the smoke open my passages to the possibility of something else.
Something other than pain. Something other than doubt. Something other than being closed and fighting.

As the smoke entered my body, I could feel it clearing the way for something else.
It used wisdom and experience to scrub clean my insides.

Cough. Tears. Trash.

I then walked with the children down a narrow path between trees and thick bush were dirt quickly changed into sand and crystal-clear ocean.

The pores on my head opened wide to let in the healing ocean water.

And as the waves beat the remaining toxins from my roots, I take deep breaths from my scalp. Pulling God down into my heals.

Floating on my back and gazing into the sky's loving eye.

Listening to the sound of water babies splashing nearby.

I smile. We are safe.

I feel Love.

Forgiveness

I see you brutha.
I see your destruction, your abandoned
children, exposed oversized faded boxers,
and guns aimed sideways.
I see, something else.

I hear you brutha.
I hear your calls from jail, your trunk
rattling, your "Bitch this and Bitch that".
I also hear, something else.

I smell you brutha.
I smell your weed and tobacco, your hair
grease, sweat, fear, and old spice.
I also smell, something else.

I feel you brutha.
I feel your angry soldier spirit, your
wordless poetry, and hushed cry.
I also feel, something else.

I taste you brutha.
I taste your Guinness Extra Stout and gold
teeth, your smoked ribs, and black n mild.
I also taste, something else.

I know you brutha.
I know your selfish twisted love, blind rage,
toxic ego, and sorted masculinity.
I also know, something else.

Something divine about you.

And so, it was. In a moment of my own healing, I found absolution. Not only for myself but for others.

Man kills man.
Man's womb was toxic.
Woman's womb was violated.
The violator was violated.
That violator was violated.
That violator was violated.

How to carry the weight of stories you don't even know. Stories that are not mine.

I was not there, and I cannot account for everyone's side nor the consequences suffered or spared.

They are not here and cannot account for my side nor the consequence suffered or spared.

The gaps in the story are too big and the assumptions are chaotic random explosions going off in my head.
Weighing me down and slowing my progression.
If you are justified, then so am I and so are we and so are they.

It's all heavy. Too heavy to carry.

So, I throw them all down in the form of words that take shape in my journal. Each story representing the purging of broken pieces from deep within me.

Faith tells me to just place the broken piece down. Let them land exactly where they are supposed to be.

Forgiveness allows me to graciously sort it without emotional limitations. It says, "there is no need to be burdened, or shammed. Lay them down with care. All of them. With care"
The ugly, the bloodied, the forgotten, the angered, the selfishness, the abandoning, the oppressed, the jealous, the pity, the insecure, the hatred, the monsters.

So, instead of burning all the broken pieces, I lay them together.
Designing a colorful patchwork that brings me so much satisfaction to rub my hands all over.
Feeling the immaculate imperfection of jagged edges and rough beginnings. Kneading the tender endings. Embracing the unsuspecting corners. Seeing the colors with my fingers. Tasting every bitter and sweet moment with my palms.

One breath I'm smiling, the next I'm crying.

Daring myself to remember.

Making sense. Making words. Making magic.

Every sentence is lightening my load. I breathe and my chest gets bigger and bigger with every placement.
Next, feeling the euphoric release of pressure as I exhale.

I don't want to take the broken pieces back home with me.   I want this mosaic.
A mosaic forged by forgiving hands.

Helping me to see that

Forgiveness was there, on the back of that tree on that cold night in the woods.
Forgiveness had to be there, in those carpet angels.
Forgiveness had to be there when the phone hung up.
Forgiveness had to be there, in the lake with all my stuff.
Forgiveness had to be there, in the bush.
Forgiveness had to be there, in the womb.
And forgiveness had to be here, now

The gentle pardon.
The softening absolve.
She, Mama, Them, and now you are excused.

We are all excused.

Open

I'm feeling gud.
The sun and I have been making love and
my afterglow is golden.
My skin, my hair, my hips, my breast, my
ass, my arms they are in a trance and
talking dirty to the world.
Whispering sweet nothings and igniting fire
after fire, from soul to soul.
We are full.
We are ready.

I'm feeling gud.
The sun is my husband and the moon is my
side thang.
I'm satisfied and secure with what I got
goin.
There's a constant jam session with Betty
and Miles Davis smoking the stage that
exists between my thighs.
We are full.
We are ready.

I'm feeling gud.
Power and Love glow like a halo from my
head all the way down to my toes.
My lower back is prematurely curved
inward, forcing my ass to catch up
instantly.

My mind and words follow suit, serving an
unexpected twist from my lips.
We are full.
We are ready.

I'm feeling gud.
A magnetic force has taken hold and magic
is her name.
I'm moving with deep purpose and lasting
gratification that wouldn't dare to die.
My head is higher, my feet are firmed, and
my spirit is holy.
We are full.
We are ready.

I, We, all of me is open

So, I abandoned the islands' sanctuary and begin my ascent back home. I'm ready because I have had plenty of time to figure this thing called life out. But just when you think you know something, you're tested.

And I knew something was waiting for me back home.

A spiritual lady told me it would not be good. She said I would meet pain, which at the time I could not imagine any pain greater than what I already knew.

She said HE would bring me to the edge of ruin.

All I hear is HE.

All I think is "Hope HE is ready for ME"

Because I am ready for whateva.

I'm ready for souls' food, R&B, Hip Hop, Jazz, and Blues.

open mikes and art exhibits.

Theatre and cookouts.

Gospel with unanticipated runs.

Dogwood festivals and activism.

Concerts.

Thanksgiving Turkey and Christmas Ham.

Long debates about Religion and Civil Rights.

My Liberation is screaming out "I am ready"

And yes "For Whateva".

I'm ready to be touched by big hands with lifelines that merge with mine.

I need passion, mystery, and excitement. I've grown bored of paradise and consistency.

My world needs to be rocked. Literally and figuratively.

Rocked like tectonic plates shifting as molten lava bubbles underneath, eventually erupting with deep moans of release.

Hot grits, shrimp, and cheese.
Cast iron skillets of cornbread.
Fall.
Concrete jungles moving fast.
Black brands and Black Jesus.
Smoothies and record stores.
Africa Bambaataa, Wu Tang, Sade.
Sage and air conditioning.
Leather.

Back home and the smoke has cleared. There is evidence of Black Excellence in the Atlanta airport.
People are rushing by with their luggage and saying excuse me with a smile.
The sound of wheels transitioning from hard to soft floors plays over and over as announcements interrupt like hype men. Just in the nick of time. In perfect sync with all the movement.

I'm home.

Bag on my back and little palms fill both hands as we make our way to the Tran where all travelers and employees intersect to share a moment of commonality.
We are all going somewhere but must wait for the Tran to stop before we can proceed.
Be it to work, to visit loved ones, to vacation or home.

We are all headed somewhere that requires a moment of pause before reaching our destination.

Some use the moment to sit in silence and rest their minds.
Others rest their feet on a bench and fumble through belongings.
Few choose to converse, quietly.
I choose to pray silently and thank God for bringing us home safely.
And to ask that my ride to the rental car lot be on-time because I'm tired of waiting.
We all hold on as the Tran comes to another stop.

She is not here.
I'm five duffle bags deep on the curb with my children and SHE is not here.
And she is not answering my calls.
The kids sit on stacked bags with their legs dangling.
Both with handheld gaming units. One playing Cooking Mama and blowing the screen for her life.
The other playing Spider-Man and engaging his whole body to swing from building to building.
High above sidewalks, street signs, and scattered treetops.

We wait.

These unreliable friends who have no sense of sisterhood.
If I were a dick, she would be here.
If I were a joint, she would be here.

But I'm not, and SHE is not here.

We wait for an hour before calling my mom's sister to give us a ride and she gladly does.
I'm home and we are jammin to Stevie Wonder's Master Blaster.
The windows to her old white Jeep Cherokee are down and we are barely touching the Atlanta highway.

We are flying.

I'm home and we are strapped in, dodging potholes and smiling crackheads in a truck full of afros, braids, locs, and various shades of chocolate.

Frankincense and myrrh.

I'm home.

I got my rental car, and I'm ready.
First stop! Back to the bush so the kids can see who's last I saw, I beat.
I'm unafraid and prepared for whateva.
Doing what I think is right.
I think I should let them know their father.
I know how deep the holes left by absent parents travel into one's essence.
And there is a familiar void growing in their bright eyes.
So, we head back to the bush, no longer burning but still filled with soldiers.

We who never forget.
We who never sleep.
We who guard what is precious.
We who have grown into something else.

Unhumbled. He appears and I am not moved.
He is not one of us. He has not grown. He has
not changed. He is the same, but powerless.
Fire and fear are no longer on his side.
The Angel has fallen from grace and he is still
unhumbled.

Ganja.

None of me is open to this.
This is not what I've come back for.

So, I go to the one place where I think I might
find what I'm looking for.

The club.

My body needs music to keep its shape.
I dress from the feet up.
3-inch strappy heels.
My almond toes peek from just under the hem of
a wide-legged blue jean that dips just below my
navel.

Button-fly.

White tank top, hoop earrings and a ponytail
made of long braids that brush the top of my ass
as I move.

We (my homegirl and I)
    No, not that one.
enter just as the DJ is reminding the crowd, that
it ain't the butterfly because oh no that's old.
He then proceeds to politely ask to see us all do
the tootsie roll.
I happily oblige, but it quickly becomes as old as
the butterfly.

A familiar sound from back on the island begins.
I'm feeling gud. I think this is it.

Old Spice

But every other moment of my wind is
interrupted by a presence from behind.
Where the hell do, they come from?
They just appear from nowhere.
They don't even ask for a dance, they just
approach and commence to dance on you.
Literally.
I stop.
Literally.
I can't.
Literally.

They leave.

I return to generating heat from every part of me.
The furnace gets hotter and hotter as Lady Saw
tells a story about what happened to her under
the Sycamore Tree. She talks of the pride and
righteousness she neva stray from. But they
can't hear her over the sound of my hips.

The boys think I'm calling them to the yard for a taste. The men do not make this same mistake. They come to celebrate liberation and survival.
Our eyes are closed, and our hearts are open as Bob Marley calls for us to move.
And we do because in this moment we are free.

Absolutely.

The fire from the bush burns within us. Causing our spirits to rise.
It is ours and we know what it is capable of.
So, we rock and sing loudly.
Some bang palms against the walls repeatedly.
Others strike a lighter and yell "more Fiyaa"!

I am home.

I am Biggie Smalls and Lil Kim.
I am Luciano and Cocoa T.
I am Mary J and Lauren Hill.
I am not Luke.
So, I am finding a place to sit my hot ass down and catch myself.

Finding the perfect spot just above the crowd where we begin pointing out cuties to each other. There are two in particular that have my attention because I'm a sucka for locs and there are only two dread heads in the entire place.

The game is to pick and get them to get.
One is just in front of me, the other is across the room.

I choose the one across the room because no man can resist my approach.
I stand and step down to initiate my magic, but before I can start my hand is grabbed and pulled slightly.
I can't move.
I can't.
Literally.

Tom Ford

Then a whisper in my ear.
Full vibrato stuns me, and my magic is weakened.
I can't hear anything he says, but I feel every word. He has my full attention.
I turn towards him, prepared to blow him off, but who can ignore Black Invictus.
His locs are soft and tame
But his presence is hard and stout.
He smells like masculinity.

He feels gud.

The game has escaped me, and my fate is in his hands.
For a moment I'm frozen and I lose track of time.
I'm afraid.
So, I say no.
No, I will not be weak and fall for some dude in the club.
No, I will not dance with you.
No, I will not be yours.
No, I will not do what you say.
No, I will not!

I mean, who do you think I am? (In my pearl clutching voice)

In the next moment, we are in his house making love.
First on the stairs.
Then on the pool table.
Next in the bed and then in the shower.

We are inseparable and everyone can see it.
But they can't see our long conversations and moments of tearful laughter.
They can see the birthday we share, but not the soul-tie that pulled us into each other's orbit.
Instantly familiar.

We are possessed by each other.
Speaking our own language.
Our stories intertwined long before we met.
We know each other.

3-inch strappy heels are replaced by 6-inch red bottoms.
Apartments by houses.
Silver by gold.
Braids by long wavy wigs.
Clear coats by acrylics.
From coach to first-class and climbing.

Oxtails, rice, and peas

I'm not falling, I'm standing on the edge of a gigantic hollowed canyon full of echoing I love U's. I'm diving in, but not too fall. To seemingly fly as his I love U's carry me.

And his I love U's make me feel gud.

He is beautiful and safe.
He is mysterious and sexy.
He is strong and loving.
He has me open for whateva.

But his Trinidadian heritage threatens to end it all.
So, we are married.

I think he might be a cheater but Whateva.
I'm still going to try and feel gud for as long as I can.

As long as I can stand to be open.

He's dead
Life has escaped him.

I'm alive.
Life lingers in me.

But he, me,
We
are all still here.

Gratitude

Move!

You are standing in the way.
The line behind you is growing longer and
longer.
The way ahead is clear.

Move!

Your dues have been paid, so why are you
still standing here looking up at the menu
as if your selection were not already made.
It's too late to change your mind.

Move!

That's what the universe said, and I knew that was him driving by and I knew what lied in that parking lot.
But we
    Yes HER.
That one.

Must leave hot plates of jerk chicken and oxtail in search of truth.
It was time I move, and I did. With all the hesitation of a newborn child going in for a breast, I got up and proceeded towards the car. Hastily we move in stealth to catch up with truth that happened to be riding down Memorial Drive in a tan hummer with chrome wheels.

I will not embarrass myself.
I am his wife.
I will no longer block the passageway.
I will move!

I choose to know. Knowing that ignorance is bliss.
I choose to move. Knowing there will be no return.

There is no unknowing what I already know.

I must move!

There is no option to stay.

Lingering has become unacceptable.

Move!

So yes, we left hot plates in pursuit of truth.
Truth that stains the cold damp wall of a long dark cave along with my thoughts. My memories. My twisted realities.
All smeared in living art along this passage.
I walk and run my fingers along its uneven surfaces as the air grows still. My feet are like the Tran in the Atlanta Airport, carrying me to my next destination. I am moving however at the same time forcibly paused before proceeding to my next destination.
But instead of praying quietly to myself, I am remembering and examining.

Moving and Knowing.

To once again see with my hands as they materialize the gospel truths of my life.
I am finding everything in its rightful place as I move out of my head and into reality.

Taking long deep breathes as colors from my life's mural are bleeding onto my palms that work their way along the depiction of the courthouse where we married. A courthouse that turns into a prison as my hands pass. And me sitting alone in a cell, waiting.

Us signing our marriage certificate and kissing before handing it to the baby mama who is revealed to be standing on the opposite side of the counter as my hand swipes over her gigantic forehead. She is laughing at me.

Us looking into each other's eyes transforms into me looking into his eyes as he smirks at the women standing behind me. They are laughing at me.

Me kissing him goodbye becomes him kissing her hello.

A wipe of my hand along an image of him lying on his stomach as I massage his back, next revealing her laying beneath his relaxed body. She is laughing at me.

Me watching his back while I'm exposed.

And She
       Yes HER.
       That one.

Was not invited here. She is truths +1.
The unintended guest. The courtesy.

One moment she is walking next to me, the next she's stepping into the painting, becoming one with the images on the wall. I continue waving my hands along the surface of the tunnel walls and remembering.
Revealing an image of me whispering into her ears then she is whispering into his.

One moment she is riding shotgun ready to defend the sisterhood, the next she is sitting in the car at a distance, watching as I confront my husband and his "cousin" alone.

One moment she is celebrating the love I have found, the next she is daydreaming of the love she has made with my husband and then...
And then
	Then I am five duffel bags deep on the curb with my children at the Atlanta Airport.

She is laughing at me.

This is not what I paid for? I want my money back.

Ain't truth supposed to be like the gospel that sets us free?
Where is the joyous tambourine and hand clapping?
Where is the Holy Ghost when you need it?
There is no choir slowly progressing down the aisle in white robes???
No glowing aura.
No naked cherubs dancing in the clouds.
For God's sake can someone please save my soul from all this truth?

It is spilling like Niagara Falls into my cup that runneth over and over again.
Crowding my thoughts and clouding my judgments.

But I can't stop. There is no return from knowing.
Knowing what has, is and will be.
One way in and one way out.
The way ahead is clear but growing darker and darker.

Trembling legs carry my weary soul towards a distant light that shines enough to reveal Mama laying on the backside of that tree.

The red impala is sitting on bricks.
The last gasp of air before the phone line is cut.

The carpet angels are rubbing off my skin.
The smiling black eye.

The dancing cherubs turning into bullets.
The bowing bodies are falling dead to the ground.

The playful man-child with a gun.
The innocent girl-child with a knife.

I'm tired and it's making me sick.
I don't sleep. I eat. I don't cry. I eat.

Lupus is crawling all over me, eating away at my skin.
I am bandaged from head to toe and unable to walk.
There's a syringe in my hip.
And a pharmacist giving me more.
The sun shines on my pregnant belly.
The moon eclipses a rejected womb.
I am alone and lying in the bed, contemplating death.

Nothing is sacred anymore. These walls are without boundaries. Knowing and revealing everything.

One way out.

Move!

My feet scramble forward.
I trip and my whole body falls against the wall.

There in the image, I am five duffle bags deep with my children in a Chrysler 300 flying down the Atlanta highway.
Barely seeing and feeling nothing.

They are excited to see their grandfather. I am numb.

One moment we are in Georgia, the next we are in Alabama.
One moment we are seemingly free, the next we are obviously segregated with the rest of the black folks in Lafayette.

I place flat palms firmly against the wall and move them down with exact synchronization.
One hand reveals schoolhouses with old textbooks, old buildings, old folks teaching and raising football players, plant workers, and hairstylist.
While the other discloses a refuge for children to explore and grow into scientists, doctors, or whatever they could imagine.
One hand uncovers a map of food deserts and redlined slums.
While the other shows historic plantations still occupied by benefactors of the enslaved.

I continue to guide my hands down the wall along paralleled lines until my whole body is lying flat on the floor with my hands still flat against the stories presented on the wall of the passage.

Confused I glance up to see something in-between that I have missed.
As I take to my feet, I notice one hand is covered in black, the other in white.
I instinctually begin rubbing them both just between the two-story boards revealing something else.

An exception.

My proud black father and his fully restored one hundred and fifty-year-old antebellum home complete with a historic plaque and servants' quarters.

It breathes. It's alive and blood runs beneath its floorboards.

The sight of its tall conquering columns reaching up from a fat-bellied porch that hugs the entire home and its gated brick driveway re-energizes me. It ready's me to move again. And I do.

I take my time to explore the crawl space with ovens for coals to heat the house.
I move from room to room counting the fireplaces in each, including the ones in the hallways.
The kids and I tap dance on hardwood floors and stairs that wrap up and around, and around again.

Art covers massive walls with black faces, African masks, and tribal statues line the hallway.
Gigantic chandlers float above every room.
The library has shelves from the ground all the way up to the raised ceiling. Not an inch is empty. Space only made for Grandma Isabell who stands watch from the mantel.

There is one dark room. It is for Billiards. Pool table, darts, board games, big-screen television, karaoke machine, disco ball, and bar.
The pool water is clear and undisturbed. The lawn is freshly mowed with track lines stretching from end to end.
It is well kept and manicured, but no one is there. Ever.

He, my father is still paying the price for its grandeur.
A price that cost him all his time.
A price too high to enjoy.
A price for us.

My hands tremble as the blood that rushes from floorboard to floorboard, wall to wall, and room to room grow restless and enraged.
Sacrifices. Bloody sacrifices made by the enslaved, the sharecropping field workers, the Jim crowed, the segregated, the integrated, the underappreciated, the underestimated, the over-policed, the over-jailed, the barefoot marchers, the voters, the blues singers, the freedom fighters. The mothers.

The fathers.

This is not a home. It is a transitional memorial that exists for me.

I am flooded with thanksgiving.

I pay homage on my hands and knees, cleaning and maintaining his declaration. It stands in inaudible poetic justice.

As proof of the exception made for me.

I am thankful for the something else that I now know. That I've always known but never registered.

For the way out.
For the paid ticket.
For the passage forward.
For the blood beneath the floorboards and the path beneath my feet.
For the knowing that all I must do is walk and be in grace.
For the opportunity to move.

And I do.

Hands moving slowly, massaging the sacrifices to the surface.

The weight of motherless and fatherless children. My sister and I, and our children rest on his back.

Hands moving slowly, unmasking a Grey pin-striped suit complete with a lavender shirt, purple tie, silk handkerchief, soft black cotton socks, and leather shoes hung in a bag just behind the closet door. Prepared by his hands. Hands that knew what he wanted to wear when

he went to join momma as she lay waiting on the back of that tree.
She made her sacrifice long ago.
He made his.
And now, I must make mine.

The laying on of hands, the healing, the grace, the miracle.
The dues paid.
The way ahead is clear.
I passed through. Rebirthed.

A new beginning.

Move!
And I did.

Death

One thing none of us can live without

None of us

Not Big Mama
Not May
Not Jimmie
Not Grand Ma
Not Aunt Ester
Not Dolly
Not Grand Pa
Not Michael
Not Alphonso
Not Mutai
Not Uncle Jim
Not Stella
Not Grand Pa Ludie
Not Our Baby Girl
Not Ulysses
Not Daddy
Not Shanice
Not Grand Ma Isabell
Not Kesha
Not You
Not Me

None of us

Rapture

The tortured, torture
The hurt, hurt
The neglected, neglect
The rejected, reject
The jilted, jilt
The removed, remove
The violated, violate
The abandoned, abandon

And he was
And he did
all of these things.

Mercy.

Not for him, but for the seeds born in the bush.
Let not the blood he spills flow over into their soil.
Soil tilled by hardened, loving hands,

Forgiveness. Grace. Exception. Sacrifice. Honor.
Devotion. Glory.

I have begun to celebrate a knowing of divine things. Things that are mystical. Things that represent a unique exception made for me. Things that allow me the option of something else.
But these things are not mine to keep for myself. They belong to the legacy I chose when I entered that womb.
They belong to the legacy they chose when they entered my womb.
The legacy that will outlive us all. The one that lives forever.

He made his choice too.
To make the pain of others palpable.
Tangible enough for him to use for his twisted pursuit of retributive justice.

He chose not to honor our legacy. He did not choose me or them. He chose vengeance.
And long after the battle was over, he chose to continue fighting. Sending bullets without a name into a universe filled with life.
Yes, you can assign a name to the metal projectile before it exits its chamber. You can tell it its' name.
But once it takes flight, it will not answer to you or anyone else.

All it knows is direction and speed.

"Tell me where to go, and I will happily serve the consequence of going there. I will not stop until something stops me.
Something.
Anything.
Be it fear, pain, or anger, I will deliver your message wherever I land. I have the power to make them all see that you indeed matter. Including you. Yes, you and everyone should know how great you are. So much that nothing will stop me until I know you are satisfied with my performance. Performance-based on my speed and accuracy. My ability to stay the course, no matter what."

"I do not miss."

"I go exactly where you tell me to go. No matter what. Because the only thing that matters is you."

He didn't know how powerful he was. But the bullets knew and that's why they were happy to oblige in his every command.
They always knew how mighty he was, but not mighty enough to avoid his own fate.
There was no outwitting his rapture.
When his vengeance met another's, the atmosphere was disturbed in the most irreparable way.
And so, where their bodies. His deviant divinity had run out.

The bullets that landed in his enemy's and the innocent.

The bullets that were dodged.

The bullets that carried love and punishments.

The bullets that once bounced from his metal frame, into his hand and shoulder leaving nothing but a scar.

These very same bullets at the will of the universe now explode like nuclear bombs throughout his body. Racing to their destination. Going exactly where they were told to go. Along the way taking particular interest in his spine.

Raging from one vertebra to next.

Screaming "Sit Down"!

And he did.

And he would, forever.

Aside from its creator, the most powerful force I know has restored balance. The universe knew exactly what needed to be done and did it without hesitation. The smoke clears and it stands justified.

Spilled blood runs to the water where it is purified.

Allowing the world to release a deep exhale in a moment of sabbath.

Divine order for the sake of Grace.

Grace that allows

The unforgiven to forgive
The misunderstood to understand
The unwelcomed to welcome
The unheard to hear
The unseen to see
The unvalued to value
The unloved to love

With this, a great rapture has occurred as we all are protected in this place.

Not just in the bush, but wherever we are.

Bye Felecia

I have many names.

*There is the one they call me in the office
and the other at home.
There is the one they call me at the market
and the other at the nail salon.
There is the one they call me on the dance
floor when all they can see is from my waist
down.
There are also the names they call me to my
face and the others when I am not around.*

Many names.

*Some make me feel proud and full of light.
Others remind me that I am a descendant of
an enslaved people and make me want to
fight.
There are the ones I answer too and the
ones I don't, depending on who calls.
But No matter the name they use, it is
conjuring a frequency of my essence
whenever it is called.*

You cast a spell and get exactly what you deserve depending on which name you use. So, don't be no fool, make sure to choose wisely. I cannot be held responsible if what you call leaves you crying

I have many names.

But only one will I take to my grave. Not the one they pay six figures a year for cause it really ain't worth a dime. Nor the one with a serial number attached cause it can't withstand infinite time.

I'll take the one that evokes a goddess with endless potential. The boundless, distinctive, euphoric cultivator. The wistful.

The one that doesn't undermine or disregard any part of me. The one that speaks to my full, mighty being. The one that most can't call, because they are afraid to summon all of me.

Except for my children. They do not hesitate to call all of me to their service. And I answer.

The rituals of a mother require adornment of walking, talking, laughing, crying, growing, manifesting altars.
Cracking the code to the right routine that fosters an individual sense of great purpose undetermined by you.
You are only a vessel and a guide fortunate to witness their independent evolution.
The reward from giving of yourself unto an extraordinary unknowing before your sun sets into the Earth.

Sometimes our sun sets early in the afternoon. Long before they have had a chance to fully awaken.
Other times it waits until they are resting before it decides to go down.

My sun had not fully risen before their awakening. They were early to rise, starting their day long before I fully peaked. And by the time I did, they were well on their way to their own destiny.

And I am scared.
Scared that I was not enough.
Enough for them and enough for me.

Have my sacrifices been bloody enough to protect us from the world?

A world that is crumbling around us. What is inhumane is subtlety amplified and mama earth is giving up on us.
We are her altar and they are mine. So, we likely share similar dilemmas.

While she wonders if she has led us to a place of self-destruction by spoiling us with her riches. Giving and giving unto use without swift consequence. Contemplating if she helped us to survive and live a life of convenience, while at the same time handing us over to our own death?

I'm wondering, have I laid a path that leads them to a twenty-first-century massa. One that sits in an office instead of a plantation home.
With his suit and tie, whipping you with his policies and procedures. Limiting you out of respect for his privilege.
Masking his racialized and gendered agenda with phony professionalism.
Providing you comfort in exchange for your soul.

No, No, No!

The exception was made for me so I must make the exception for them.

My ritual must satisfy not only their bellies but also their ego.
So, I lead them to a sanctuary where young black minds can grow. Straight to Historical Black Colleges where they are allowed to lean so far into their blackness that it becomes obsolete. Requiring them to ask what else?

Giving them the opportunity no other college on earth will allow without limitation of color. Without implying they are anything other than their peers. Anything other than destined for greatness.

"I know you're black. I know they have abused you because you are black. I know black can sing, dance and entertain and that's great. I know black is marginalized, overlooked, and misunderstood. I know black is strong. Fierce.
I know black is King and Queen.
YES, Yes, Yes you are black.
Now.
What else?
Because everybody here is black. So how are you going to differentiate yourself here in this place of greatness?
Who are you really? Where is your voice? How does it really sound? What do you really think?
How does the altar which BE you manifest its blackness into something great?
It can be many things. Anything you can imagine. Greater than they ever imagined.
How? "

And their heads are higher than mine and I am thankful for it.
Inspired by their climb, I converse with myself.
I say
"I know you're black. I know they have abused you because you are black. I know black can sing, dance and entertain and that's great. I know

black is marginalized, overlooked, and
misunderstood. I know black is strong. Fierce.
I know black is King and Queen.
YES, Yes, Yes you are black.
Now.
What else?"

Overnight I became dissatisfied with the name they call me. It conjures servitude, fear, and the limitations they place upon me.

This sacrifice is bloody as hell.

I've been subconsciously beat into submission. My eminence is suppressed. I am settling for suburbia at the cost of my own self. I am physically sick and dying. They will have my life. They do not value me. I am not fulfilled. I cannot manifest my blackness into its greatness here. They won't allow it, yet they continue calling that name. Casting a spell of compliance, acceptance, consent, and accession.

Wait.

I too am an altar, and the rituals of my ancestors are still burning in me.
I am still evolving. My sun has not set into the earth and I am thirsty.
So, I leave a six-figure salary, benefits, and that name behind in pursuit of something else.

I am a writer.

And all they could say is "Bye Felecia"

I did not answer.

Surviving

*I just ran smack into the realization that I
am alone, and it does not feel good.
It feels like sinking silence that leaves you
dizzy and nauseous.
Stillness without breath.
This is death.
There is no heartbeat, or blood circulating.
There is only nothing.
And what does one do with nothing?*

Nothing.

I lied.

There is something to do. Think.

And there is one stream of thought revolving in my weary head.

I am alone and if I call, no one will come. My life is hanging onto death.

Because that is what I know and that is when they will come. When I die, they will all show up and tell stories of how much they loved me, how I was there for them, how I made them laugh, and how they regret not being present in moments like this. Moments when my thoughts recline back and go to the sunken place in search of demise.

How loving she was.

But not lovable. Not worth coming when she calls.

She fine.

She a'ight.

She doesn't need anybody.

She got it all under control.

She is strong.

She is a survivor.

Alone in my house built for a family.

2 adults
2 children (1 boy, 1 girl)
1 dog
Perfect

2 adults need 2 sinks in their bathroom, a large closet, and plenty of drawers to store their stuff.

1 child needs a place to find his independence. So, there is a bedroom and bathroom in the basement with restricted privacy.

The other child needs a place to await her turn. So, the upstairs hallway has another room and bathroom.

1 dog needs 1 fenced in yard.

2 cars need 2 garages.

6 seats at the table, 8 in the family room, 8 on the patio, 5 in the sunroom, 9 in the entertainment room, 2 at the bar.

1 lonely, slightly disturbed occupant, counting the consequence of surviving.

Taking a tally of my accomplishments and trying to figure out how much matters to me, and me alone.

0

Nothing matters to me, and me alone.

I have done nothing for myself but sacrifice for others. Continuously paying retribution for not being enough. Finding swords to throw myself on, so I can pull through and survive.

I lied.

I have also proven how strong and courageous and loyal I am. That makes me happy. To know that I have put myself in a position that drastically lowers the chances of me becoming a distraction from the lives of others. Their lives of which I value more than my own.

I only live so they do not have to suffer the loss of me.

I've done nothing for myself but survive for others.

Congratulations! You have successfully suffered in silence and made use of toxic positivity. Your perfection of small talk and inclusion has given you the advantage. Padding your body with layers and layers of fat so no one can hear you screaming from the inside.
Well done!

But even in dejection, I know this cannot be an ending. The story must go on until there is something for me in it.
Something for me first.
Survival offers hope to keep going, but it is not enough until I am.

It offers a resting moment. Again, the much-needed pause before exiting the Tran and proceeding to the next destination. A time to reject, reflect, grow, and heal.
But these moments pass by too quickly and before you know it, I've thrown myself onto another sword before the completion of the process.
Never making it pass rejection.
Never fully completing self-discovery.
Never growing or healing.

Just surviving. Until now.

Now in the silence of nothing I see.
This is no accident. With pure intent, I avoid my souls calling for long-term exclusive self-satisfaction.
For something that will not leave me with nothing.

I have been programmed against that which manifest from a place of self-worth and self-love.
That which requires emotional work and awakening.
That which requires me to put down my own self-sabotaging sword, pick up a pen, and write.

So, I start over by first rejecting all those things that fail to serve my greater purpose.
Then reflecting on all the things that do.
Next leveraging these things to promote my own growth.
And last, but far from least, I am healing.

This feels good. Like a blossoming beginning to something wonderful, that is not nothing.

It is everything and so am I.

I am loved.

Thriving

Every morning as I sit alone in my sunroom sipping coffee.

5 seats. 1 optimistic occupant.

A Red Cardinal sings from the patio just outside the window.

Be lifted up from the inside out so you can sit on high.

Mother yourself and be the gentle guidance you need.
Reassure yourself and tell yourself how proud of you, you are.
See your flaws and love them with all of you.
Give unto you unconditionally.
Forgive yourself unconditionally.
Sever those cords and be free.
Move with the intent of your own prosperity.
See the ordinary trouble disguised in unique circumstances.
Don't be fooled. They are not precious, and they do not need guarding or protecting.
Lay down your suffering.
Not yourself.

Be lifted up from the inside out so you can sit on high and fly with me.

My response.
Keep singing and I might just do that.

For years, the red bird has been trying to convince me that I can fly.

One day I raced up interstate 75,
one moment I was in Alabama where it was dark,
the next in Georgia.

Two hours later the sun was up, and I was at work just north of Atlanta.

Eight hours later I was racing back down interstate 75.

I was alone, tired, sick, and weary. My divorce almost final, my sister absent as usual, my father buried and me needing to move closer to work and away from his grand memorial that I could not maintain on my own.

I was a zombie racing against the clock to pick up my children from the after-school program in another time zone when a cloud of red birds began to pass over the highway.

In complete synchronization, they dove down towards the road just ahead of me. Soaring wing to wing, leaving me without space to pass. I had no choice but to enter their flock and drive right through.

As I did the repeated crashing of their bodies into the car could be heard over the music.

I'm startled but undeterred as I have to pick up the kids on time or they will charge me a dollar for every minute I'm late and I cannot afford a dime.

Once the kids are gathered, I arrive home and begin to inspect the damage. Apart from a scratch or two that may or may not have been caused by the birds, there is nothing of concern. That is until I look under the hood, where there is a lone red cardinal. Lying there on the radiator was the vivid remains of the setting sun. His feathers captured every tone of its radiance as it makes way for a moonlit sky. His unbothered plume gently rested over his body as if they were unattached. Understanding there was no need to hold on to something that simply belonged. I wished someone were as faithful to me as those feathers were to that cardinal. To be there even when I'm falling to my death. To not let me go alone. Be my protection and strength. To behold me as sacred and carry me up. To be to me what you are to no one else.

To simply belong and honor that.

I've always believed that nothing happens without reason. My mother-in-law agreed. I called all the way to Trinidad to tell her the story of the red birds. I could hear her smiling through the phone.
In her native twang, she said, *"It means all will be well child. Your father is with you clearing the way ahead and you shall have your victory."*

The path is narrow at times, and at other times steep, but clear it was and clear it will be.

As I sit listening to the Cardinal's song, I consider all the other wonderful things ahead. I am contemplating so many possibilities besides death. Seeing my life without padding. Taking time to do what I love and being open to receiving it.

I'm healing myself. Believing in myself.

At some point, my suffering became more important than my survival.

And my survival more important than my wellbeing.
But now, I am being called to make decisions from a place of purpose, not duty.
There is an internal voice beckoning me to heal so I can experience life without second-guessing what good it has for me.

To live abundantly and without absence.
To be completely honest with myself and others.
To enter every moment without hesitation.
To fully be present.
To vibrantly move from second to second.
To celebrate wins and failures.
To transcend trauma and grow over and over again.
To fly and sing like the spirit of the red cardinal that set its sun so that I could rise.

To Thrive

Freedom

I put it all on the line for a dream.
In return, I am granted a taste of freedom
and it's a wonderful life.

Every day is Saturday.
Morning coffee.
Song with birds.
Delicate, loyal Pitbull eyes watching me.
Jazz on vinyl.
Research in bed.
Deep consideration before determining what to do with my day.
What to wear and how much time I want to spend getting dressed.
More coffee.

Everything rest when I rest.
Outside of my dreams, nothing has happened as I slept.
So, I awake to pick up exactly where I left off.
No time is needed to close the cabinet doors, pick up the trash, push in chairs, or tidy the couch pillows.
Everything is right where I left it. So, I need not look for what my memory can't find.
No questions about breakfast or complaints of the temperature.
It smells like incense and sage.
Nothing is empty. Except for the trash can, all containers are full. The laundry detergent, the soap, the orange juice for mimosas, and almond milk for more coffee.

During the day I sit in the back of coffee houses, bleeding onto pages. Ignoring my phone as my fingers are preoccupied with a mission to press keys in formation to the sounds of Anderson Paak.

"Yes, Lawd!"

Imagining myself cooking grits and rolling his spliff at the same damn time. In an apron, with my booty all-out cooking bacon.

It's a whole entire vibe in the back of the coffee shop where I am surrounded by stiff white elites and Stepford Wives who have no idea what they are looking at. I really don't care but they are suffocating my creative process, so, I expand my quest for coffee into the city where I can breathe. Where my bejeweled locs and tattoos fade into a mash-up of culture and class. Where there is space for my magic to work.

During the night I am usually lost in reality television waiting for someone to catch a fade for my enjoyment.
Trolling the chat rooms with strangers who are just as petty as I am.
We come together in celebration of trivial moments with a great consequence to those who take life to seriously.
We share our memes and gifs in honor of the minor assault on black women and negligible reflection of reality.

It's great! Not!

But on this night, I find myself in the club toasting with associates and chanting anthems of two generations younger than me.
I'm a mess and a savage.

Layers of stress have been peeled back revealing a mighty brick house.
Unimpressed, temptress, and seductress.

He is still everything I remember. Black Invictus wraps himself all around me.
Damn his hair smells so good.
Once again, he has captured me, and my mind is idle. This is dangerous.
But I'm free to do as I please and nobody is telling me no.
Nobody can. Nobody will.
This moment feels so right.
Even though I am walking backward in the passage. Trying to rewrite the story that has already been told.
Attempting to repair what has already been fixed.

We are back.

As if no time has passed. No love lost.
Our minds, bodies, and spirits are present and entangled.
Jubilation.
Inspiration.
Melodic bliss oozing from our every movement.
We can't speak without smiling.
We can't touch without smiling.
We can't think without smiling.
We can't glance at each other without smiling.
Our love is resurrected like roots into the future.
We BE elevated. Exploring our freedom.
This is good medicine.

It's a super soul Sunday morning.

We awake eye to eye and smile as our bodies lay
on top of the sheets.
Doors open.
The smell of incense and sage linger.
Exhale as his nakedness exits the bed in a rush.

Let's eat, but he casually declines.
Exposing that he must return home to his wife.
There is a ring cutting off the circulation of the
beluga whales' hand.
I'm laughing.
This shit is hilarious.
Not only am I the other woman, but reality
television is real.

Sunday morning tea.
Freedom can be petty as fuck.
Hence the Stepford Wives.
Hence this moment.

I'm obviously not finished exploring my freedom.

Abandonment

Everything is something.
Some things never amount to anything
But teaches you something.
So, everything is something.

And there was something about him.
Something that came just when I was being forced to confront what I know and what I don't know.
To push the envelope and explore deeper inside.
To challenge my safe status quo.
It was time I acknowledge what I see.
Acknowledge what I sense.
Acknowledge what I know.
And I know exactly what it is.

Nevertheless, I cannot escape it.
Even though I want to, there seems to be no getting around this.
I want to abandon this need to be attached to something.
Anything that places limits on me. I want to be free.

So, I do the work. I pray. I acknowledge. I affirm. I meditate. I study. I dance. I fast. I burn. I supplicate. and I am stronger and better for it.

I pass every test.

They try, but I will not allow myself to fall for something that doesn't meet my needs.
Something that does not serve my greater self. Not just who I am today, but who I will become and who my children will become. And their children. And their children's children. And so on.

They come fine and rich. They are creative and bold. They are many things, but not for me.

But then there is him.
Something in him I am latched to.
I just need something from this one.
No clue what it is, but I cannot pass GO until I
know.

Everything is something.
Some things never amount to anything
But everything teaches you something.
Yes, Everything is something.

This day is fabulous and so are my friends.
They are pretty on purpose.
Two of the most beautiful men I know showed up
in full disclosure of who they are.

Of African descent.
Fashion-conscious freedom fighters.
Joyful noisemakers.
Laughter conjurers.
Boundary pushers and spiritual warriors.
Gay.
PERIODTT

6 feet or greater in height and gorgeous.
Sharp leather jackets.
Crisp white T-shirt.
Beads.
Jeans. Destroyed.
Leather boots. Laced. Kinda. Confident.
One royal Kufi, black with gold trim.
One royal Gele, black and white adinkra pattern.

Two flesh born angels.
We were fly. In ever since of the word.

I dressed from the head down.
First gathering my locs in a bun to rest just above my forehead and slightly to the right.
Toping it with a large brimmed black fedora.
Next a large African red, black and yellow beaded necklace.
Solid black one-piece Harlem jumpsuit.
Jean jacket. Destroyed.
Adidas.

Black on Black Range Rover.

It was a night for art and activism. A celebration of differences. In this polarized world where everyone is forced to fit into one of the limited pictures or else.
Else you were a mistake.
Else you were unwanted.
Else you were unloved.
Else you were dangerous.
Else you were a threat.
Else you were wrong.
Else you were fragile.
Else you were ugly.
Else you were confused.
Else you did not belong here or anywhere.

This day provided one big fluid picture without rules or boundaries that everyone can fit in.
And we (my angels and I) did not want to fit. We refused and so would everyone else there.

Before arriving, I imagined there would be waves of love and beauty dancing through the crowd as prisms fill everyone with light and sound.

Senses stimulated. Thoughts provoked.
Knowing challenged.

I never imagined that on this day fluidity and boundaryless acceptance would show up in an unsuspecting package.

But first, we must park.

Black on Black Range Rover.

The only parking available was down a dark road in the back of the venue. An old man sat in a chair with one dim light shining over his head.

"$20 bucks," he said.

What if this is not his lot?
What if this is a scam?
What if?

"Is this your lot?" I ask. He tells me he's a preacher (furthering my suspicion) and the white building to his back was his church.

"hmmm huh"

He went on to tell us that all would be safe, and he would be out there all night to make sure nothing happens to the vehicles in his lot.

Side-eye
Okay

but I am still nervous, so we approached a package, I mean police cruiser, blocking off the street just a few yards away.
It's too dark to see more than his white teeth and eyes, but his kind voice was enough.

My thoughts come and go quickly.
Why was he so nice and pleasant?
Doesn't he know that police are mean and hard?
Don't he see how they drag us in the street?
Suffocate and shoot us?
What's really in this package?

The first impression was dismissed and lost until after the festival that lived up to everything I imagined, and we were approaching the questionable parking lot.

Black on Black Range Rover.

The old man and the package where still in their place. Waiting. Nothing had changed.
I opened the door but instead of getting into my

Black on Black Range Rover.

I turned around and went back to find out exactly what was in the package.
I'm not sure why? What am I looking for? But my feet continue to move in that direction, and I didn't care to stop them.

There is something about him. I got to know what it is.

What's in the package?

"Are you single?"
"Yes"

We exchanged numbers, the next morning I awoke to a "good morning" text accompanied by a head, shoulder, and arm shot. Then a full-body shot of him in uniform. He's cute, but I'm feeling rushed.

I responded "good morning" hesitation.

My thoughts come and go quickly.

Is he just trying to get inside of me like everyone else?

I know this game. Send a pic, get a pic. Starts with a headshot, and before you know it, they are sending you dick pics expecting to see your breast.

I send a head, neck, and shoulder shot. Then nothing.

Quickly establishing that first base was not on my radar, yet. As a matter of fact, I would not even get out of the dugout until I felt Safe.

Completely safe.

That night he called.

He is so pleasant. This is new.

He wrote a book and published it.

He is an artist. He is open and ambitious.

He has deep passion and critical thinking skills.

I like that.

Virgo.

He is perverse and masking pain beneath a fuckboy persona that concerns me.

I'm intrigued.

I'm guarded on the outside.
But on the inside, my thoughts come and go quickly.

We would not make babies. Instead, we would make stories. His would make me blush, mine would make him wonder.
He's not the typical guy that I would be attracted to, but he is satisfyingly my type. I think.
Maybe he's too judgmental. Too picky. Too bossy. Too detached. Too unbothered.
Maybe I'm too careful. Too spoiled. Too independent. Too unsatisfied. Too empathetic.
Maybe we are both too scared.
Scared to choose.

It's making me uncomfortable, so I hesitate on the outside.
But on the inside, I want him to push down the door and pull me out of myself.
I want to experience boundless, infinite moments with him.
I want intimacy that stretches and challenges me.
I want considerate companionship that takes care of my heart.

We have plans and I'm waiting. He doesn't call. He doesn't text.
And when I do, he is at work.
He is either irresponsible or incredibly rude.
On the outside, I'm nonchalant and doubting his character.
But on the inside, my thoughts come and go quickly.
We could be living in a house on the top of the hill.
Making love with the French doors to the balcony in our room open as the rain falls and the city lights peek up in the far, far distance.
We could be nurturing ourselves and our children. Together.
Laughing and crying. Together.
Finding our way. Together.
We could be taking care of each other.
And feeling safe. Together.

We have plans and I'm waiting. He doesn't call. He doesn't text.
And when I do, he is on his way to work.
He is selfish and conceded.
On the outside, I'm telling him all about himself.
But on the inside, my thoughts come and go quickly.
We could be in our swimsuits, bathing in the sun and eating breakfast on a floating table in a clear infinity pool just off the coast of Guadeloupe with nothing but ocean, sky, and devotion.
Us intertwined on a hammock as I read aloud and warm my foot against his leg.
Him peacefully existing on the verge of sleep

as our breaths and heartbeats harmonize while the waves sing a massaging lullaby.
We could be wearing our feelings and taking on the world. Together.

But

He is challenging me and I'm doubting myself.
He is letting me down. But I'm holding on.
He is clearly unavailable. But maybe I'm just not making my intentions clear.
He is not really interested. But maybe I'm just being too guarded.

Before you know it, I'm bending.

And there it was.

Me, like when I was a child holding on to something that was not there.
And the more obscure it becomes, the tighter I grip.
Painting pictures in my head.

Afraid to let go.
Letting go could mean missing out on my opportunity to have what I really need.
Or even worst, ending up with nothing.

Afraid to hold on.
Holding on could mean missing out on my opportunity to have what I really need.
Or even worst, ending up with nothing.

I block, I unblock.
I follow, I unfollow.

Finally, I am unsatisfied.
I'm sadder than my fear.

So, I do the work. I pray. I acknowledge. I affirm. I meditate. I study. I dance. I fast. I burn. I supplicate. And I am stronger and better for it.

My thoughts come, but this time they stay.
They are in the shape of my mother.
They are not over yonder. They are right here.
Touching me. Holding and filling me up with everything.
She holds my heart while I cut the cord and release all attachments.

What I know is.

All packages are empty until someone puts something in them.
Here I am putting in and he's pulling out.
I keep revisiting the package. Closing and opening it to see if he has left anything for me. Anything at all.
Shifting the bubble wrap from side to side. Shaking and listening.
Reaching and digging. Reaching and digging.
Dumping out its' filing. Climbing in to examine with a black light.

There is nothing.

So, I replace the bubble wrap, reseal the package securely to prevent anything else from getting in, and with a thick black sharpie, I write with freeing conviction.

"Wrong address, please return to sender"

Now all I have to do is put it in the mail...

Processing

The laws of science teach us that lightning strikes 10 seconds after the rumble of thunder, But never in the same place.

The laws of my life beg to differ because as I hear the roar, I also feel crippling shock at the same damn time.

I am smoldering, I am alone.

And according to scientists, I should find relief in this paralyzed state. Because chances are, I will not get hit again.
But no, I'm hit over and over until I'm blind and numb.
Until it doesn't matter.
Until my childhood fantasies fade and my faith dwindles.

I'm being tested

So, I do the work again. I pray. I acknowledge. I affirm. I meditate. I study. I dance. I fast. I burn. I supplicate. And I am stronger and better for it.

But I'm not satisfied with strength.
Strength helps me to bear, not understand.
Strength helps me to endure, not grow.
Strength is powerful, but strength alone is
vacant.

It needs courage, wisdom, compassion, patience, gratitude, direction.

I got so much I want to share.
Don't I deserve?
Ain't I worthy?
Don't I matter?
Haven't I suffered enough?

I mean who the fuck am I?
And what in the hell does this life want from me?

Processing

Apocalypse

Apocalypse or revelation.
An unveiling or unfolding of things not
previously known.
Things that cannot be known without an
unveiling.

Today.
I can still smell the combination of age and
devotion inside the church.
Hear the sound of Mama's voice forcing its way
across the slanted exposed beams and into
hardened hearts.
Hands clapping, robes dancing and spirits rising.
I am that church.

Today.
I can still feel the swift shift of every fiber in the
carpet as I lie on my back and rake my arms and
legs up and down in Daddy's hallowed house.
Feel the Angel's breath along the backside of my
neck.
hear them whisper comforting words as I
daydream.
I am that house.

Today.
I can still taste warm blood and feel it thicken as it dries on my lip.
I flinch at protruding thorns as they gravitate into flesh and drag along its form.
See the bushes' resilience and its constant burning.
Crackling flames, floating ambers, and radiant light.
I am that bush.

Today.
I can still see Grandma Isabell's hat lean into the battle beneath that tent.
Warrior spirits paused and waiting for her command.
Quietly challenging, covertly asserting loyalty and fierce love.
Reclaiming muted truth to give it back it's voice.
I am that tent.

Today.
I can still hear the rumble of blood rushing underneath the floorboards of Daddy's ole memorial.
Climbing the walls and spilling into my veins.
The metaphysical cage of immortal sacrifices.
Granting me passage.
I am that memorial.

Today.
I can still hear my first breath after the hummer passed.

Tearing my heart to pieces, seizing all movement from my chest and fancying vengeance.
Swallowing God's iodine into a grieving underbelly.
Unveiling
I drove that hummer.

It was my own will that called for truth to free me and it showed up just on time.

Saturn has returned and Leo is rising.
I am reborn and my true feelings blossom from rich soil mixed with the remnants of an ever-present past.
From pain, from love, from joy, from loss I create izms and cyphers.
Conjuring todays' knowing.

And Today, I know

If he does not love his hair.
He cannot love your hair.

If he does not love his skin.
He cannot love your skin.

If he does not love his nose.
He cannot love your nose.

If he does not love his back, his feet, his shoulders, his arms.
He cannot love your back, your feet, your shoulders, your arms.

And if you do not love yourself
You could hold his blues in your heart
forever.

You see Blue ultimately wants to slow the human engine and bring forward tranquility. It wants you to let down your guard and trust.

To do so, it may present itself as a calming ocean or a faithful sky. It may even find the confidence to appear in a suit that exudes reliability. It sometimes lends itself to berries, morning glories, lullabies, and hummingbirds. Florida crayfish, Hydrangeas, and butterflies. Just gets you to feeling good. All to convince you to relax and stop being alert.

But there is another side to Blue.

It gets sad and cries out through saxophones, pianos, voices, and bases.

It can also captivate us with hypnotic flames from gases that warm, but also pollute. And can also maim and destroy.

Come to think of it,
lullabies rhythmize lies.
Berries can be poisonous.
Suits are uncomfortable as hell.
People drown in the ocean all the time.
Hydrangeas stink.
Crayfish have cancer-causing mercury.
And hummingbirds are aggressive.

Yea Blue is complex and heavy. It has good intentions that sometimes pave the road to hell.

However, I know hell ain't a place, it's a frame of mind that can haunt you right here on earth.

And knowing that Blue is a hue that cannot be created by the mixing of other colors, like all the primary colors, it is on its own abundant and complete.

Blue is just more committed to my peace of mind than red or yellow. While yellow works to unleash my creative energy and red my power, blue takes on my inner peace by any means necessary.

Blue is the color of my struggles and lessons.
Truth and purpose.
Freedom.

Blue doesn't want me to live in hell, it just drags me through it sometimes to accomplish its goal.

They, We all have our blues. Trini has his and I got mine.

I don't want Trini's Blues, because mine alone is enough.

Body

Dear Body,

I was watching you in the mirror the other day and couldn't help but notice how beautiful you are.

Your curves are unexpectedly moving unlike any I've ever seen. Taking risks that others wouldn't dare take. Effortless collaboration with a solid frame and as a reward for all its sweat equity you have power beyond imagination. Your breast are empaths. Responding to the unspoken words of the world around.

Their nipples like the rings of an ole tree, seasoned and filled with wisdom. They are telling stories and sustaining life by giving of themselves.

I spent all day trying to figure out how one ass can be as captive as a solar eclipse. A beautiful distraction that takes my breath away as you perform magic before my eyes. Building a house out of bricks with no mortar and no stone. Just you standing as your foundation takes shape. Enchanting thighs. Mesmerizing hips. Oh, what a magnificent form and architecture. You should be worshiped.

Sincerely,
Your first love

Voice

Dear Voice,

You should be heard. You are the only thing powerful enough to distract me from that ass. You are translating emotions into words that no man dares to mute. Your mind takes laps around the world at every period, apostrophe, comma, and semicolon. I'm left in disbelief of your whimsical charm. Fascinated by the way your lips hug and hold each other as they move like a romantic Angolan kizomba dance. You create sound from a place that I did not know existed. I don't even know what to call it. Authentic, Genuine, Passionate, Kind, Generous, Pure, blessed. I don't even know where it is going but I'm more than glad to go there and be forever. I am better after every conversation. You lift me and shift what I know. To listen is to be anointed.

Sincerely,
Your first love

Eyes

Dear Eyes,

You see beyond the imagination. Exposing truths and telling stories without words. You make me believe. Erasing doubts and restoring faith. I am humbled by your ability to find just the right moment and the right position to awaken deep understanding. Through you, I am liberated. Take me with you. Wherever you may go I am willing to follow. Even to the darkest places where there is nothing to see, I want to be present and feel. I wanna know and see everything that you know and see. What do you watch behind closed doors? What conversations are you having? What secrets do you hold?

How precious you are to hold the responsibility of being a window to one's soul. I hope you never lose your sparkle or fight back tears because you should be unbound by the capsules of which you exist. You should be free.

Sincerely,
Your first love

The Beginning

About the Author

 B.A. Buie is a big-hearted introverted African American poetic and descriptive writer from North Carolina. After living in and outside of the United States, she landed in Georgia where she was also raised. Recently she escaped a career in Corporate America just in time to pursue her dream of being a writer.

As an awkward suburban empty-bester who has dedicated her life to raising the most amazing children in the entire world that now attend Morehouse and Spelman College, she is determined to live out the remainder of her days exploring (both world and self), loving, inspiring, laughing and writing arts that will not only entertain but challenge status quos, provoke meaningful conversation and stimulate personal growth. B.A. Buie intends to carve out space for all women of all backgrounds, race, status, and class to join her on a quest to raise above their struggles and do more than survive. Thrive.

Made in the USA
Columbia, SC
11 September 2020

19901996R00085